PRAISE FOR
BAREFOOT DREAMS OF PETRA LUNA

- A 2022 Pura Belpré Honor Book
- New York Public Library Best Book of 2021
- A Texas Bluebonnet Master List Selection
- NPR Best Book of 2021

★ "Dobbs's wrenching debut, about family, loss, and finding the strength to carry on, illuminates the harsh realities of war, the heartbreaking disparities between the poor and the rich, and the racism faced by Petra and her family. Readers will love Petra, who is as strong as the black-coal rock she carries with her and as beautiful as the diamond hidden within it."

—*Booklist*, Starred Review

★ "With vivid and poetic imagery and artfully balanced narrative tension, Dobbs's assured writing blazes bright, gripping readers until the novel's last page."

—*Publishers Weekly*, Starred Review

"Viscerally relevant to contemporary readers."

—*The Bulletin of the Center for Children's Books*

"The parallels between past and present government corruption and violence make this historical fiction that is as relevant as ever...A timeless and timely tale of one girl's journey to save her family and discover herself."

—*Kirkus Reviews*

"This beautifully written and exciting story of a family fleeing during the Mexican revolution offers a new perspective in historical fiction."

—*School Library Journal*

"*Barefoot Dreams of Petra Luna* will draw you in with its raw, evocative setting, and Petra herself will win your heart with her courage, resourcefulness, and unwavering love for her family. Lyrical, heartfelt, and deeply authentic, this book will stay on your mind long after you've read the last page."

—J. Anderson Coats, award-winning author of *The Many Reflections of Miss Jane Deming*

"What hunger would you endure, what history would you sacrifice, what hazards would you brave to lead your family through a war? Petra Luna's incredible odyssey in pursuit of her 'barefoot dreams' is as vital and perilous and hopeful as that of today's dreamers, who still set off across the desert seeking a better life in America more than a hundred years later."

—Alan Gratz, *New York Times* best-selling author of *Refugee*

"Alda P. Dobbs's stunning debut novel, set during the Mexican Revolution, recounts one girl's determination to save her family and follow her dreams. Inspired by the author's great-grandmother, *Barefoot Dreams of Petra Luna* is as breath-taking as a shooting star"

—Laura Resau, award-winning author of *Tree of Dreams* and *The Lightning Queen*

"A brilliant and authentic historical novel about a young woman's struggle for freedom. Petra Luna's dream will fill your heart with courage"

—Francisco X. Stork, award-winning author of *Illegal*

ALSO BY ALDA P. DOBBS

Barefoot Dreams of Petra Luna

The
OTHER SIDE
of the RIVER

The
OTHER SIDE
of the RIVER

Alda P. Dobbs

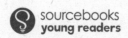

Published by Sourcebooks Young Readers, an imprint of Sourcebooks Kids
P.O. Box 4410, Naperville, Illinois 60567–4410
(630) 961-3900
sourcebooks.com

Cataloging-in-Publication data for the hardcover edition is on file with the
Library of Congress.

This product conforms to all applicable CPSC and CPSIA standards.

Source of Production: Worzalla, Steven's Point Wisconsin, United States
Date of Production: July 2022
Run Number: 5026116

Printed and bound in the United States of America.
WOZ 10 9 8 7 6 5 4 3 2 1

FOR MY MOTHER. THANK YOU FOR TEACHING ME TO

LOVE MY CULTURE, MY LANGUAGE, AND ALL PEOPLE.

AND FOR ALL IMMIGRANTS WHO ARE

FORCED TO ABANDON THEIR HOME IN

PURSUIT OF A BETTER TOMORROW.

"El que persevera alcanza."

—Dicho Mexicano

"One who perseveres reaches."

—Mexican Proverb

PROLOGUE

Thousands of us—the poorest of the poor, the underdogs—choked the narrow bridge and begged for our lives to the gatekeepers, and despite the sun glistening over the smooth river below us, everyone, including me, believed it was the end of our lives.

The *Federales*, mounted on their horses, raised dust as they galloped downhill toward us. Their chase across the desert, full of violence and destruction, was ending here in Piedras Negras at the edge of the Río Bravo. Their fury and rage would soon be upon us, and our lives now lay in their hands.

A blur of people pushed and shoved around me. With my back against them, I gripped the bridge's iron rail. My little sister, Amelia, was beside me, and my baby brother, Luisito, was in my arms. I pressed them close to my body, hoping it'd be enough to keep them alive. Terrifying screams ripped through the crowd until the thin gap between the tall swinging gates grew wider and wider, making the other side of the river clearer and clearer. My eyes narrowed on the open gate, on our passage to freedom, on our escape from death, and I ran.

For as long as I lived, I'd never forget the smiles on the American soldiers' red faces as they guided a parade of terrified, broken people into their land. Later that day we found out that after thousands of refugees had crossed the bridge, the Americans had to shut the gates once again, perhaps to keep the revolution from spilling over. My heart ached for the people who hadn't made it across, who, despite their long journey, had remained on the other side of the Río Bravo. Their fates lay in the hands of the Federales.

My siblings and I had made it across, and when Abuelita found us standing under the American flag, I counted my blessings for having crossed. But still, Papa and my cousin Pablo were not with us, Mama was dead, and the revolution in Mexico still raged.

A strange thing happens when a country fights itself.

There are no winners or losers. One side may claim victory, but in the end, it's a loss for everyone. It's like two parts of a single body fighting each other. If the head claimed victory over the feet and destroyed them, then the body could no longer walk to explore better places. If the feet destroyed the head, then the body could no longer think nor plan for a better future.

My country had been fighting itself for three years, and there seemed to be no end in sight. My family and I had fled before the deep rift that tore our homeland apart swallowed us whole. And as I stood under a new flag with my bare feet grasping a new soil, I wondered about this new land. Had it ever fought itself too? How had it survived? Was it strong enough and able to provide the safety my family and I had walked across the desert for?

All I knew was that I was grateful this new land had opened its gates when we'd most needed it.

OCTOBER 1913

FORT DUNCAN, TEXAS

one
AN EAGLE'S PASS

It was early, dark still, when crashing sounds startled me awake. I sat up amid the darkness, tense, ready to run. My heart thrashed inside me. Had I heard a cannon blast?

"It's okay, *m'ija*," Abuelita whispered. "It's thunder. We're in a new place, a safe place. Go back to sleep."

My eyes adjusted to the darkness and to the sudden lightning that flashed through the narrow gaps of our tent. We *were* in a new place, a new home. We were on the banks of the Río Bravo and right in the middle of a refugee camp.

My stomach soon awoke, and the nausea rising from its emptiness made me swallow hard. It was our third day in America, and despite having escaped the revolution in Mexico, hunger still had a tight grip on us.

We'd heard the American soldiers were scrambling to find ways to feed us. There were nearly seven thousand people who had crossed the border bridge the day the Federales came to Piedras Negras. Many of us had run across with nothing but the ragged clothes on our backs. Those who'd managed to bring a little bit of food, like cactus pads or stale tortillas, had since eaten every last bit.

We'd been told we'd get food, but no one knew when.

I made out Abuelita's figure as she sat on a wooden crate near the tent's entrance. She squeezed at her elbows, her shoulders, and every joint that complained about the cool, moist air.

"Abuelita," I whispered. "Do you need me to rub your hands?"

"No, m'ija. I'm fine," Abuelita said. "I want you to rest and be ready for work at sunrise. We're in America, and we can't let tomorrow go to waste."

I lay back on the dirt floor and curled into a ball with my bare feet tucked under my skirt. Next to me Amelia and Luisito slept, and outside, the rain poured. I reached into my skirt's pocket and pulled out my black rock, my baby diamond—the only thing I had left of Papa.

My black rock was a small piece of coal from when Papa worked at the mine, and every time I squeezed it, his words rang inside me just as clear as the day he gave it to me: "When life's problems squeeze you hard, you grow stronger. You grow up to shine like a diamond."

The harsh wind continued to lash against the canvas walls of our tent; I lay still despite the deep hunger nagging fiercely at my gut. I tried to clear my mind just like Abuelita had said to do when you wanted to listen to nature. On this night, I intended to listen to the wind. Perhaps it brought news of Papa and his whereabouts in Mexico. The wind knew of the sacrifice Papa had made seven months ago. It knew Papa detested the Federales and had refused to join them at first. The wind saw when the Federales put him in front of a firing squad for his defiance. It had heard my screams and felt my pain the moment I saw him blindfolded with rifles aiming at him. The soldiers pulled me away, and Papa agreed to join the hated Federales to spare me the pain of seeing him killed. The wind knew it all.

So I remained still. I wanted the wind to tell me Papa was safe fighting for the Federales or that he had managed to escape them and join the *Revolucionarios*.

I squeezed my black rock hard and pushed every thought out of my head. But the wind said nothing, it brought nothing no matter how much I remained still. Instead, it blew wet and cold, as if coming from a strange, new place.

Morning sunshine poured through the tent's narrow slits, and voices heavy with concern broke the morning silence, just as they had the past two mornings. They were from people stopping by, giving us names, and asking if we'd heard of their missing mothers, fathers, sons, or daughters. The refugee camp had become a grapevine of information for people seeking loved ones. Abuelita always gave the same response: "*No, lo siento.*"

This morning I heard Abuelita say, "*Ay, Dios,*" and she gasped. I rushed to the tent's entrance, fearing Abuelita had bad news about Papa.

Abuelita, with a hand over her heart, spoke to a man whose tent was nearby.

"*Cuándo?*" Abuelita asked him.

"Last night," said the man. "They pulled a large pine

box out of the tent, with the dead woman inside. I was told it was smallpox."

"And what about her children? Are they well?" Abuelita asked.

The man shrugged his shoulders. "The gringos aren't letting anyone come near the area. They have everyone there in *cuarentena*."

Cuarentena referred to the forty days sick people were required to remain home. In the camp, that word brought fear of sickness, fear of being sent back to Mexico, back to the revolution, and a fear of death.

The man left, but Abuelita's shocked look remained.

"I don't know what's going to kill us first," she said, "hunger or smallpox."

"Maybe I'll find work today and can buy us some food," I said. "Can you give your blessing?" I bowed my head, and Abuelita made the sign of the cross over me, whispering a blessing.

"Abuelita," I said, "I heard last night that a group of people here at the camp want to go back into Mexico and retake Piedras Negras. I think everyone here is too hungry and scared of smallpox."

Abuelita put an arm around me. "*Mira*," she said and

raised a bulgy finger toward the river, pointing at Mexico. "The revolution is across the Río Bravo. It's behind us. But our battles with hunger and now smallpox—those are still with us. Don't get any wild ideas about joining that group. We need you here with us."

I reached for the ends of the purple scarf around my neck. Often, when I touched my scarf, I thought of Marietta—a captain of the rebel forces and the toughest woman I'd ever met. After Abuelita, my siblings, and I had fled our village in Mexico, Luisito had become very sick, and Marietta helped save him. She took our family to a rebel camp, and thanks to her, we were spared from death. Yet, as much as I wanted to cross over and join Marietta's cause, and as much as the hunger twisted my stomach and made it want to eat itself, I still had a promise to keep. A promise I'd made to Papa to keep our family safe.

I thought about my dreams too, but at this point, neither side of the river seemed to offer a good chance of making them come true.

"I'll stay put," I said to Abuelita.

I walked away, thankful Amelia and Luisito were still asleep. I hated to see them awake and hungry.

I passed rows and rows of the same canvas tents that dominated the camp. Their dull color matched the mood on people's faces, mostly women and children, who sat outside desperate for food. At the end of the city of tents lay an open field where hundreds of people huddled in small groups. These were the refugees who had reached the camp after all the tents had been taken up. They lay out in the open without even a shrub to provide shelter from the wind and rain.

I walked up the dirt road, away from the camp, rubbing the chill off my arms. Other lonesome souls trekked far ahead and far behind me, all of us with our heads bowed against the wind.

Our camp had been set in the outskirts of a town with an English name that everyone pronounced as *igle pas*. Like Piedras Negras across the river, I'd been told this town's name also had a meaning. It meant *el paso del águila*—the eagle's pass. The Mexican flag carried a proud eagle on its center, and I wondered if we were the eagles who'd stepped into this new territory.

When I reached the center of the town, the fast and colorful automobiles didn't impress me like on the first day I'd come there. They now seemed loud and annoying. I had walked most of the streets in town, and none were paved with gold or sprinkled with diamonds like I'd once imagined. They were dull and muddy and made from packed earth like the ones back home.

By midday, I had knocked on at least fifty doors, and my knuckles stung. I offered to chop firewood, herd sheep, milk cows, clean stables, or scrub floors, but everyone shook their head and said the same thing. "*No hay trabajo*. There's no work."

I stopped before heading back to the camp and took a moment to stare out at the wide, gray river. Federales guarded the Mexican side with rifles, each standing about fifty steps from each other along the river.

I loosened my scarf and filled my lungs with the air sweeping in from Mexico. It didn't ease my mind nor my hunger pains, which had grown into ferocious growls that jabbed at my gut and spread queasiness all over me. The *Americanos* had opened their gates and provided shelter, but the food wasn't coming. No one knew when or *if* we'd be fed. And if the smallpox became worse, would we all be sent back to Mexico? It'd been three days since our brush with death at the bridge, and things were once again dire.

I glanced at the ground, and something shiny stood out. I picked it up. It was a smooth, bright green wrapper with a strong smell of spring within its folds—a soap wrapper. I stared at the words on it, and my heart leaped when I recognized a few letters from my name. I folded it and tucked it next to my baby diamond.

I hadn't found work, but I had found something that reminded me that my dream to one day read and write still burned within me.

I heard the wind again. Was it talking to me in a different language, in one I was yet to learn? Was it whispering things from a different place or a different time? Telling me of future encounters or friendships to come?

I hushed my mind once more, took a deep breath, and let the wind speak to me. And though I couldn't understand it, I clung to the sense of peace and hope it brought.

two

BARE FEET

Abuelita sat on a crate outside our tent while Amelia, sitting cross-legged next to her, poked at the ground with a stick. Our neighbor, Doña Juanita, stood near them. She carried a sleeping Luisito over her shoulder.

Abuelita called Doña Juanita a godsend. She had nursed Luisito since our arrival at the camp, and thanks to her, Luisito's cheeks had turned rosy again. She seemed to enjoy feeding and caring for Luisito, and Abuelita said it probably soothed her sorrow of having recently lost her husband and infant son.

As soon as Amelia saw me, she waved her short stick in the air at me. "Did you find any work?"

Her question caused neighbors to stop what they were doing or peep out of their tents. When I shook my head, everyone went back to their business. Abuelita frowned and continued talking with Doña Juanita.

"Sit here," said Amelia. She used her hand to sweep a spot next to her. My knees trembled as I sat.

"We got to eat a little," whispered Amelia, as if sharing a secret. "Doña Juanita gave us two tiny pieces of cacti. She said they were her last." Amelia's small fingers reached into the hem of her skirt. "I saved you some."

Amelia placed a dry piece of cacti no bigger than a fingernail on my palm. I fought hard to keep my hand from shaking and quickly popped the parched cacti into my mouth.

"Do you like it?" asked Amelia, wide-eyed.

I nodded and forced the green stalk down my dry throat. It dropped into the pit of my stomach like a single raindrop falling into the open desert.

"I found something," I said, reaching into my pocket.

"A diamond?" asked Amelia. "Are the streets covered with them?"

"No," I said, handing Amelia the wrapper. "The streets here are the same as back home. I think it's a soap wrapper. I remember seeing them in the store back in Esperanzas."

Amelia unfolded the wrapper and ran her small hand across its smooth surface. "Why didn't we ever buy any?"

Abuelita looked over and chuckled. "Because soap like that costs as much as four dozen eggs."

Amelia brought the wrapper to her nose and cracked a smile. "It smells like the fancy ladies from back home." She glanced at it once more before rubbing it over her arms and her neck. "I want to smell nice."

"M'ija," said Abuelita, "it's going to take more than a shiny piece of paper to make you smell fancy."

"Your grandmother's right," said Doña Juanita.

Amelia shrugged her shoulders and continued to rub her arms.

"Amelia," I said, "stop it. You're ruining the paper,"

"Do you want to smell fancy too?" asked Amelia.

The question annoyed me. "Of course not, but I want to keep the paper and know what it says one day."

Abuelita gave an eye roll and turned to Doña Juanita. "I told you, this girl and her barefoot dreams. She's obsessed with learning to read and write."

Doña Juanita gave a light chuckle and shook her head.

A tiny pang of anger crept inside me. "What's funny about wanting to learn to read?"

"It just doesn't make sense," said Doña Juanita. "It's good to have dreams, but those kinds of dreams, well, they're bound to make you miserable. Think about it. What good would it do to know how to read? You have no books, you can't afford the newspaper—a dream like that is pointless."

I figured it was best to keep my mouth shut and let her speak her mind, because no matter what, she wasn't going to change mine.

"Look," said Doña Juanita, "I used to work for a rich family, and I've learned that the rich have problems of their own, just like us poor people. But if you get the ideas and desires of the rich, you'll end up with their problems too. You'll end up with more than you can handle. Just keep your life simple."

Abuelita went on to explain to Doña Juanita what she meant by barefoot dreams, of how dreams like mine weren't meant to go far like us barefooted peasants. My insides twisted, making my hunger pangs more painful.

Before I could say anything, Doña Juanita turned to me. "Your grandmother is right, Petra," she said.

I shut my eyes to keep from rolling them.

"But don't let the rich fool you," Doña Juanita said and looked over at Abuelita. "There's no shame in being barefoot, right?"

Abuelita shook her head repeatedly.

"You see," Doña Juanita continued, "when our bare feet touch the ground, we're one with the earth. We become rooted to our past, our culture, and our traditions. When we fill our heads with nonsense, like wanting to read or write, we detach ourselves from what's important."

"But learning to read is important to me," I said.

"You're wasting your time," said Doña Juanita.

"I am not," I said, jumping to my feet. "You have no idea *who* I am or *what* I've been through."

"Petra, *más respeto*," Abuelita scolded. "Show respect."

"I know exactly who you are," said Doña Juanita. "Look around you. Look at your skin, your feet. Despite that fancy scarf around your neck, you're like me and everyone else in the camp. We're all *indios*. We work hard with our hands, and after a long day of labor, a few tortillas and beans are all we can hope for." Her jaw tightened. "I hate to say this, but I think the only reason you want to learn to read is because you're afraid of work."

"I'm not afraid of work!" I blurted. I turned to Abuelita, who stared at the ground in silence. It burned me inside that she wouldn't stand up for me and tell Doña Juanita all I'd done in our journey. I had to speak up for myself.

"You see these bare feet?" I said, my voice breaking. Doña Juanita glanced down at them. "These bare feet outran the Federales," I said. "They crossed the desert and got my family and me to America. I am not afraid of work, and if anyone is foolish, it's you for believing that my barefoot dreams won't go far."

"Petra!" shouted Abuelita.

I turned away and bolted toward the river as fast as my weak body would allow. I wanted to be away from the stranger who believed she knew me and from Abuelita, who hadn't stood up for me. I didn't want them to see my tears. I didn't want them to sense my frustration that no matter how hard I worked, my dreams seemed to move further away.

three
THE SIGN

The morning sun was well above the horizon, and I lay on the dirt floor with my eyes shut. My body was too weak to move and my heart too numb to care about a new day.

Amelia came into the tent. "Petra," she said. I kept my eyes shut, hoping she'd think I was still asleep, but it didn't work. Amelia repeated my name and sat beside me.

"I saw a sign today," she whispered into my ear. "No. I saw two signs."

I remained motionless.

"Petra, I'm talking to you." Amelia tugged at my shoulder. "I know you're awake."

I opened one eye. "What kind of signs?"

Amelia knew what I meant. The signs I liked had written words. The signs Abuelita liked served as revelations.

"The kind Abuelita likes," said Amelia.

I shut my eye again and turned to the other side.

"Petra." Amelia ran around and sat in front of me again. "These signs are real."

"Then go tell Abuelita," I said with my eyes still shut. "She'll be excited to hear about them."

Amelia used her fingers to pull one of my eyelids open. "But I want to tell *you*."

I sat up with a heavy sigh. "Go ahead. Tell me."

Amelia smiled and sat up straight. "Yesterday, I made a friend here at the camp. She has a rooster, and this morning we fed him and took him to the river to get water. The whole time, he didn't crow at all. But as soon as we carried him inside her tent, he crowed this many times." Amelia held three fingers up to my face. "That means there's good luck coming our way."

I shook my head. "The rooster probably doesn't like being inside a tent. Or maybe he felt scared. I'd crow too if I were surrounded by a bunch of hungry people."

Amelia sucked in a deep breath and dropped her shoulders. She eyed me as if wondering how to convince me.

"What was the second sign?" I asked.

Amelia reached into the hem of her skirt. "Open your hand."

I put my hand out, and Amelia dropped a small copper coin in it.

I brought the coin to my eyes and squinted. This coin was different from all the ones I'd seen before. On one side was the profile of a bearded man. On the other were a pair of wheat leaves framing a group of words.

I shot up, staring at the coin. "This isn't a sign. This is money. Where'd you get it?"

"I found it by the river," said Amelia. "It's good luck. It means we're going to get more money later."

"Maybe, once I work," I said. "For now, it means we can buy food."

Amelia stood up. "How much food?"

"I don't know. Let's take it to town to find out."

"Let's take it now," said Amelia.

I stopped her before she could run outside.

"Don't tell Abuelita we found this," I said. "At least not for now. I don't want to get her hopes up."

Amelia glanced up and down at the buildings, the automobiles, and the fancy people walking past us. She opened her eyes wide as if not wanting to miss a thing.

We stopped in front of a shop where I'd asked for work at least three times in the previous days. I had tried to buy food with the few *centavos* I'd brought from Mexico, but the lady behind the counter, who spoke Spanish, said she wasn't allowed to take Mexican money. Her boss had told her the revolution had made centavos worthless.

"Is this the place?" asked Amelia. She pressed her face against the shop's window and used her hands to block the sunlight.

"It is," I said and pulled out the small copper coin.

We went inside and saw the same lady I'd seen before. Though her clothes weren't as fancy as the rich ladies' back home, they were nice. She smiled as soon as she saw me.

"*Buenos días*," she said. She stepped down from a stool with a feather duster in her hand. "Any luck finding work?"

I shook my head. "No work, but my sister found this." I handed the lady our coin. "How much is it worth?"

"It's a penny, one cent," she said with a frown, handing back the coin. "It's not worth much, but..." She put the duster down and browsed up and down the shelves. "The least expensive thing we sell, other than the barrel candy, are potatoes, but each costs two cents. Then there's corn, we sell that for..."

The lady paused, and then her face lit up. "You know what," she said. "Take your penny to the nixtamal mill down the street. You'll get a lot more for it there."

"A nixtamal mill?" I asked. Nixtamal was corn that had been boiled in lime water. Abuelita used her metate to grind it into *masa* for tortillas. And though I'd heard of a flour mill and a lumber mill, I'd never heard of a nixtamal mill. "What's that?"

The lady chuckled. "It opened last year. It's a place where women take their corn to have it ground. They also make tortillas. Your penny will go a lot further there." The lady handed my copper coin back. "*Suerte.* Good luck."

I thanked the lady, and Amelia and I rushed down the street to find the mill. We ran inside and stopped short at the line in front of the counter. The five women standing in line, some as young as me, carried buckets of cooked corn. Clattering noises rattled the tin roof.

"Why is it so loud here?" asked Amelia, putting her hands over her ears.

I stood on my toes and looked over the counter. I bent and spoke into Amelia's ear. "It's machines that grind the corn here, not metates." I pointed at the two machines standing about ten steps behind the counter. Each spewed steam from the back and rattled as they ground the corn.

Amelia stepped out of the line and stretched her neck to catch a glimpse of the action. The lady behind the counter took the buckets of nixtamal and dumped them into what looked like a giant tin funnel sitting atop of the machine. Another woman then gathered the masa, the dough, that had been spat out of its side and placed it back into the bucket. Amelia's eyes followed the buckets. Some were returned to the owners waiting at the counter while others were carried to a row of women sitting across large *comales*, griddles.

Each woman put a small ball of dough between their hands and patted a tortilla into shape before placing it on the griddle. Their soft, gentle claps were drowned by the noises of the machines. Amelia turned to me and smiled like she'd seen a street paved with gold.

I couldn't wait to tell Abuelita about this place. As much time as she'd spent on her knees grinding corn on the metate, she would be the most grateful for the nixtamal mill.

"Can I help you?" asked the lady at the counter.

I placed my coin on the counter and spoke loud over the clattering. "How many tortillas can I buy with this coin?"

The lady glanced at the coin, then her eyes quickly shifted to Amelia and me. A gentle smile formed on her lips as she picked the coin from my hand. She crouched behind the counter, and after a moment, came back up with a large piece of paper folded in half. She handed it to me, and inside the fold was a thin stack of tortillas.

"Thank you," I said. The small stack steamed in my hands and spread warmth all over me. Amelia shoved herself between the counter and me and scrambled to reach for them.

"Wait," I said, holding the tortillas high. "Let's go outside, and I'll give you one. I promise."

We ran across the street and sat on the sidewalk. I placed the warm stack on my lap and unfolded the paper. My heart pounded as I counted ten tortillas. I peeled one from the stack and, in a swift motion, rolled it up and handed it to Amelia. She gobbled the whole thing before I could roll up a second one. Still chewing, Amelia stretched out her hand, ready for another.

"Eat slower, Amelia," I said, handing her a second tortilla. "We only have a few."

Amelia took it, and as I began chewing on mine, she'd already devoured hers. She remained quiet, though, and glanced at me with hopeful eyes.

"We'll save some for Abuelita and Luisito," I said. "And Doña Juanita too." Doña Juanita's words from the day before still stung, but I thought of how good she'd been to Luisito.

"Here," I said. "Let's split this tortilla between us."

Amelia raised her hand to reach for her half when I caught sight of the tiny pink blotches on her forearm.

"Amelia," I said, gasping. "What's that on your arm?"

Amelia puckered her lips. "I don't know," she said,

"but look at this." She raised her sleeve to show me the flesh under her upper arm, which was completely covered with raised blotches. I nearly dropped the tortillas.

My eyes scanned Amelia's face, and then something on her neck caught my eye. Gently, I pulled her tangled hair to the side. Just like her arm, Amelia's neck was pink and blotchy.

"Ay, Amelia, why didn't you tell me earlier?" My hand reached for her forehead. "Do you feel sick?"

Amelia chewed and shook her head. "I feel fine."

I was relieved that Amelia's forehead felt cool to the touch. But even if the rash wasn't smallpox, there could be trouble. If the American soldiers saw it, we'd be sent back to Mexico, back to the revolution, back to the Federales. And if the rash *was* smallpox, then death had crossed the border and was trying to catch up to us on this side.

"We should get back to Abuelita. Maybe she can look at it and tell us what it is." A sunken feeling filled my stomach, and I no longer felt hungry.

As Amelia and I approached the camp, we could see groups of American soldiers building something along the edge. We'd soon be walking past the soldiers, and the thought of them noticing Amelia's rash tightened my insides.

I glanced toward the river. Perhaps we could go around and enter the camp near it, but we'd look suspicious trying to avoid them.

My heart raced. I reached for my purple scarf, but it was much too small to cover Amelia. I had nothing else on hand to hide her rash—no shawl, no serape, no nothing.

We got closer to the soldiers, and I could see beads of sweat dripping from their red faces as they swung picks and shoveled dirt. Some soldiers positioned posts into the freshly dug holes while others connected the posts with barbwire.

"Why are they putting up a fence?" asked Amelia. "Is it to keep the Federales away?"

"I don't know," I said, looking past the camp to the river we called el Río Bravo because of its deceiving depths and ferocious currents. If the river was fierce enough to stop the Federales, why would we need a fence?

I turned back to the soldiers and tried not to make

eye contact with them. I quickly pulled Amelia toward me and, using my fingers, combed parts of her hair to the front, trying to hide the rash on her neck.

"What are you doing?" Amelia asked.

"Hush. I'll tell you later." I wrapped my arm around Amelia, and in an embrace, I scooted her toward me as we continued to walk. With my body and my arm, I hoped to hide as much of her rash as possible.

Two soldiers smiled at us and moved out of the way to let Amelia and me walk through.

I avoided making eye contact and held my breath, and as Amelia and I walked past them, I felt their glances on us. I waited to hear one of them call out. But all I heard was the wind and the sounds of their picks digging into the earth.

I counted ten steps without turning back.

The wind blew steady.

I counted ten more steps before letting myself breathe again. And just as I did, I heard a man shouting from behind.

four

GREEN EYES

I squeezed my eyes shut and froze, feeling my heart drop into my stomach. Though I didn't know the language, I knew the soldier had shouted a word that meant *stop*.

The soldier called again, louder this time. I took a deep breath and opened my eyes before turning back.

To my surprise, the shouting soldier chased after a man, a refugee like us, who was walking away from the camp. The soldier continued to call out to the man until he caught up to him. He said something to the refugee, and with his arms, he motioned for him to return to the camp.

Relief swept over me. Still, my legs felt as flimsy as cooked strips of cacti.

Amelia pulled away from me and counted the posts

being put into place. Near us, a group of refugees stood silent, watching the fence go up.

"I bet you the fence is to keep wild animals out," said Amelia. "Like coyotes or mountain lions."

I took a deep breath. "Who cares about the fence?" I said. "Right now, we have to find out about your rash."

We found Abuelita sitting outside the tent. I handed her one of the tortillas from the thin stack, and she quickly rolled it up.

"Amelia," I said, "show Abuelita your arm and your neck."

Abuelita put her tortilla on her lap, and the crease between her eyes deepened as she inspected Amelia's arm. She ran the tips of her fingers over each blotch. "*Te dan comezón,* m'ija? Do they itch?"

Amelia shook her head.

I crouched next to Abuelita. "You don't think it's..." I hesitated to say the words aloud. I was afraid a neighbor could hear them and report us.

Abuelita didn't answer, but the long breath she took in told me she too was nervous. She glanced at Amelia's neck and asked, "Have you been playing around any *zumaque*?"

Amelia shrugged.

I glanced at the river. Maybe Abuelita was on to something. Maybe Amelia had come across poison ivy. "Amelia, you said you played with your friend and her rooster down by the river this morning. Can you show me where you played?"

Abuelita turned her head toward the tent's entrance and said, "Juanita, come grab a tortilla and take a look at this."

My insides twisted. I wish I'd known Doña Juanita was inside our tent before I said anything about Amelia's rash.

Doña Juanita came out carrying Luisito over her hip. To my surprise, Luisito didn't ask to jump into my arms. Instead, he shifted his little head to match Doña Juanita's, as both stared at Amelia's rash. I sucked in my breath. "Is it bad?"

Luisito began babbling as if trying to explain something. This made Doña Juanita laugh. She then turned to Luisito. "Is that what you think it is?"

It annoyed me how lightly Doña Juanita was taking this. "Is it smallpox?" I asked, raising my voice over Luisito's babbling and Doña Juanita's laughter.

"Dear God, child," said Doña Juanita, looking around. "Don't say that too loud." She switched Luisito to her other hip. "Not long ago, I worked for a family whose little girl got the exact same blotches every time she used perfumed soap."

I remembered Amelia with the green soap wrapper the day before. Her rash was in every spot where she'd rubbed the wrapper.

"Don't worry," Doña Juanita told Amelia. "It's not smallpox at all."

I nodded with a sigh of relief. For the first time, I felt I could trust Doña Juanita.

"I heard the Americans are planning to vaccinate us all soon to keep the smallpox from spreading," Doña Juanita added.

"What's does that mean?" asked Amelia.

"It's when they prick you with a small needle and give you medicine so that you don't get sick."

"Does it hurt?" asked Amelia.

Doña Juanita shook her head. "Not as much as getting sick from smallpox."

"Or as much as getting sent back to the Federales," I added, pointing my chin toward Mexico.

Amelia stared out across the river. Her eyes narrowed on the federal soldiers standing guard.

"If I get the medicine now," Amelia said, "will the rash go away?"

"No," Doña Juanita said, glancing at the river. "But if we wash it with water and find herbs to put on it, it may help clear it up."

Doña Juanita and Luisito ate their share of tortillas, and afterward Amelia and I joined her as we headed toward the river. As we walked, I glanced at the fringes of the camp and noticed more fence posts had been raised. Barbed wire connected most of the posts, and in the gaps that had yet to be connected, American soldiers stood guard, armed with rifles. That's when it dawned on me: The fence wasn't meant to keep the Federales or the animals out. It was meant to keep us all in.

Fear crept inside me. How were we supposed to find work or food? What if the Federales decided to cross the river to get us? We'd be trapped with no way to escape.

We reached the river. Not far from us downstream, a group of women washed clothes among the boulders. Their young children splashed in the small pools of water near them.

Amelia and I knelt by the river's edge to get sips of water. I kept my eyes on the Federales across the river as I cupped my hands and drank enough water to trick my stomach into feeling full. Doña Juanita walked ahead with Luisito to find herbs for Amelia's rash.

Suddenly, the blasting sound of a train horn made everything around us tremble. My eyes searched for the sound. It came from a locomotive near a tall, narrow train bridge. It appeared to have just stopped. Steam spewed from the sides, and its horn blasted a few more times. As I wondered where the train had come from, the women near us screamed. They scooped up their children and baskets and ran off, leaving behind the soaked clothes they were washing. Where were they running to? Or who were they running from?

I snatched Amelia's hand and ran to Doña Juanita, who carried Luisito close to her chest as she raced toward us.

"Why is everyone running?" I said, catching my breath. "Is it the Federales? Are they on that train?"

"I don't know," Doña Juanita said. Her eyes were wide and frantic. "*Señora*," she yelled to a woman running near us. "What's happening?"

"Los Americanos," the woman shouted back. "They're bringing food."

"Food!" Doña Juanita's face broke into a smile. "Petra, run to the train now before they run out," she said. "I'll drop off Luisito, grab my basket, and meet you there." She turned and ran off.

"But we don't have a basket," Amelia shouted after her.

"We'll find one," I said and tugged on Amelia's arm. "*Vamos!*"

Amelia and I ran along the river and reached the growing crowd near the train. The stench of sweat, of damp clothes, and of hungry and exhausted people hit me as I shoved myself into the crowd.

"Grab on to my skirt," I shouted to Amelia over the loud crowd. "And don't let go."

Amelia tried to nod, flicking her eyes at the people shoving her side to side.

Everyone stretched their necks hoping to get a better look at the boxcar that had begun rolling its wide door open. We pushed through the crowd, dodging elbows and slowly inching our way to the train car. My eyes scanned between people's muddied feet and behind us, hoping to find a lost basket, a sombrero, or anything to help us carry the food.

Amelia and I finally reached the boxcar, and an American soldier, wearing his olive-green uniform but no hat, stood atop and greeted us. His big eyes were as green as our shiny soap wrapper. He held up two large scoops of corn and said something in English with a bright smile on his face. I grew nervous not having a basket and turned to Amelia. Her eyes flicked between the soldier and me.

Without thinking, I grabbed the bottom of my skirt and stretched it out to the front. The soldier laughed and poured four scoops of corn over my skirt. He said something in English as his eyes showed approval. He then turned to Amelia, and she did the same.

Amelia and I made our way out of the crowd with nervous giggles and took quick, tiny steps toward our tent, our new home.

My face burned hot the closer I got to our tent. Was it because I was starting to shine like a diamond? Perhaps. Or was it because people could see our bare legs? Maybe. The truth was that, for the very first time since Mama's passing, I felt happy. We had a new home and enough food to fill our bellies for a while.

five

THE ANNOUNCEMENT

In the early darkness, Amelia's eyes reflected the glow of the makeshift brick stove outside our tent. We sat on crates and watched Abuelita turn over the tortillas that were beginning to puff up like big toads. The autumn breeze swirled around us, carrying smells of corn, beans, chili, and roasted chicken.

It'd been almost two weeks since the train had delivered its first supply of food. Every morning, each family got a batch of firewood and a healthy ration of corn, sugar, coffee, beans, flour, lard, and one whole chicken. For the first time in my life, I'd eaten meat every day. My family had eaten so well that Amelia was convinced the extra food had helped Luisito take his first steps without anyone's help.

Doña Juanita had been right. The Americans began vaccinating everyone in the camp soon after delivering the food. The week before, my family and I had all gone to the hospital tent and received our vaccines along with a piece of paper. We were told to keep the paper as proof we had been vaccinated. Even Luisito had his own certificate. To everyone's relief, no one had been sent back to Mexico. Nobody wanted to return despite the Federales' promise not to hurt anyone who went back.

I looked into our tent and could see Doña Juanita curled up with Luisito, both fast asleep. It'd been a long day for the two, with Luisito learning to walk and Doña Juanita keeping up with him. I'd never seen Luisito so happy, and his closeness to Doña Juanita troubled me. Ever since Mama's passing, good things in life had come in fleeting moments. This too, I was afraid, could come to an end soon.

The next morning, I began my chores earlier than usual. I made five trips to the river to fetch enough water for the day, and after sweeping the inside of our tent, I sprinkled water across the earthen floor to keep the dust down. As I finished, Doña Juanita came into the tent carrying the food rations. Her breathing was shallow like she'd been running.

"Have you heard?" asked Doña Juanita.

"Heard what?" I asked.

"The rebels," said Doña Juanita. "They chased the Federales out of Piedras Negras last night."

Abuelita, carrying Luisito, stuck her head into the tent. "The Federales are gone?"

"At least in Piedras Negras they are," said Doña Juanita, sorting out the food. "They're making an announcement at noon about how the Federales ran without firing a single shot."

My heart leaped.

The sun was high in the sky when Amelia and I squeezed ourselves through the growing crowd surrounding the back of the food train. We had volunteered to go listen to the announcements and bring the news back. Now we were close enough to see the three men overseeing the crowd from the caboose platform. You could breathe the excitement in the crowd. I hoped, deep down inside, to hear the revolution was over.

One of the men, short and stout with white hair and a mustache, wore a dark uniform with a gold badge attached to his chest. He was the immigration official who made the camp announcements in English. The man next to him, also short and stout, was a Mexican man with a fancy suit and a thick, black mustache who translated for the official. The third man was an old American soldier. He was tall and slender and always stood quietly behind them with his hands behind his back.

"As some of you may know," said the translator. "It's official. Piedras Negras is now under revolutionary control."

The crowd exploded into cheers. Men and women shouted, praising the revolution and yelling, "*Viva Mexico! Viva Pancho Villa!*" I reached for my purple scarf and thought about Marietta. Every part of me wanted to join in the jubilation, but the thought of Papa, forced to fight with the Federales, stopped me.

As the cheering settled down, the Mexican man continued translating, "This morning, the international bridge was reopened, and you now have two options." He paused while the official spoke in English then started translating again.

"One of your options is to return to Mexico." The crowd remained quiet, waiting to hear the second option. "The other is to remain here in the United States," said the translator. "If you decide to stay, we will continue to provide food and shelter until you're hired by one of the many contractors who will visit the camp tomorrow. Once hired, the contractors will pay your way to your work destination." The immigration officer spoke a few words before the translator went on, "The work available is in construction, track laying, meat-packing, farming, mining, and other labor jobs."

"We urge everyone to decide soon whether to stay or leave," said the translator, as whispers flowed through the crowd. "You'll have to decide soon, because the camp will shut in one week." The crowd's soft murmur turned into an outcry. Amelia and I turned to each other with wide eyes.

The translator raised his voice over the clamor. "*Calma. Silencio,*" he said and repeated this until the crowd was calm. "There are plenty of jobs for everyone in the camp, including women and children, but you have seven days." The translator raised seven fingers over the crowd. "You have seven days to determine your fate, and anyone without work next week will be promptly deported."

The translator's words, *plenty of jobs for everyone*, made my heart swell with joy. Abuelita had always said the gods decreed our fate and sent signs to guide us. This time, I was going to choose my fate. I'd soon get a job, work, take care of my family, and go to school. And who knew, maybe even Amelia could go to school too. Ever since I'd learned to write my name in Mexico, she too had wanted to learn this magic.

"Are we going back to Mexico?" asked Amelia.

"No," I said with a wide smile. "We're staying here and getting a job."

six

A LONG NIGHT

"Abuelita! Abuelita!" Amelia shouted as we entered the tent. "Petra got a job!"

Abuelita shot to her feet with a wide smile. "You got a job, m'ija?"

I chuckled and shook my head. Doña Juanita, lying next to Luisito, kept quiet as if nothing had been said; her eyes were fixed on Luisito, who slept beside her.

"I don't have a job yet," I said. "But the contractors are coming tomorrow morning. Maybe we can all go and see if we can get work."

Abuelita and I turned to Doña Juanita. Again, she showed no interest, but before I could speak, Abuelita placed a finger over her lips, motioning for me to keep quiet so as not to wake Luisito.

That evening Abuelita, Doña Juanita, and I sat in front of our tent to talk about the announcement while Amelia and Luisito slept inside.

"I'm not staying," Doña Juanita said, shaking her head. "I intend to go back."

"Why not reconsider?" said Abuelita. "Maybe you can come with us. Luisito has grown attached to you and—"

"I've grown attached to him too," said Doña Juanita. "Why don't we all go back instead?"

"Back to Mexico?" I said. "We can't go back. Our home and village were burned down. We have nothing to go back to."

"We'll go to my mother's village of Santa Clara in Guanajuato," said Doña Juanita.

"What if that village has been destroyed like ours?" I asked.

"Santa Clara is a tiny village. I doubt anything's happened there," said Doña Juanita.

"Is that where you were before coming here?" I asked.

"No, I was in my late husband's home in Torreón. I'd been there for a year when the revolution broke out. I tried going back to Guanajuato, but the road was shut, and I was forced to come here."

Ever since arriving at the camp, I had learned of many places in Mexico. Some people came from places near the coast and ate things I'd never heard of, and some even spoke Spanish different than me. But the revolution was the same for all of us. In some places the Federales had been in control, while in others the rebels had claimed the land, only to switch power from one to the other repeatedly. Our hunger and suffering were also constants that swept the country.

"I'd rather stay here," I said, "I don't want to go back and starve or be killed by the Federales in Mexico."

Doña Juanita gave a sigh. "You know, I've met people who have come to America, and life here is not as easy as people think."

I looked at her, puzzled. "It can't be harder than what we had in—" Luisito's sudden cry interrupted me.

"Go see to your brother, Petra," said Abuelita.

I hesitated. I wanted to stay and convince Doña Juanita that America was the best option for us.

"*Andale*, Petra," said Abuelita, cocking her head toward the crying.

"Yes, ma'am," I said under my breath.

I walked into the tent and carried Luisito over

my shoulder. I sat near the tent's entrance, hoping to eavesdrop, but Luisito's fussing made it difficult to hear what was being said. He settled down after a few moments, but by then the conversation had gone silent.

I pulled back the entrance flap just enough to peek outside and saw Doña Juanita leaning toward Abuelita with her hands clasped together. I then heard her whisper, "It'll be good for everyone, señora."

I wondered what they talked about and pulled the flap farther back.

"I promise to do my best," Doña Juanita continued. "If you give me Luisito, I promise I'll—"

"No!" I shouted, jumping out of the tent. "We can't give you my brother." Luisito, still in my arms, woke and wailed.

Doña Juanita stood with round, nervous eyes.

"He's not a puppy we can just give away," I said, rocking Luisito.

"Petra, go back inside," said Abuelita.

"No," I said and glared at Doña Juanita. "She has no right to take Luisito away from us."

Luisito squirmed and stretched his arms toward

Doña Juanita and yelled, "Eeh-tah, eeh-tah." This upset me even more.

"Petra." Abuelita's tone was firm.

Doña Juanita put her hand over Luisito's back. "It's all right," she said, trying to soothe him.

Instinctively, I pulled Luisito away from her and stepped back. I could feel hot tears streaming down my face.

"Petra," Doña Juanita said. She placed her hands over her heart. "I promise I was going to talk to you about this, but I thought it'd be best to talk to your abuelita first."

"It doesn't matter who you talk to first," I said, "the answer is no. You can't take him."

Doña Juanita bowed her head and nodded. "I understand, but Petra, your grandmother... she's getting older, and her health isn't good. And Amelia—she may have to work along with you to help make ends meet. Who's going to watch Luisito then?"

"That's up to me to figure it out," I said.

Doña Juanita stared at Luisito and then at me. Moonlight gleamed over the sad lines across her forehead, and her eyes appeared damp. "For now, I ask that you think about it," she said. "Think about your future and about how much Luisito needs a mother."

Abuelita nodded.

"There's nothing to think about," I said, my voice breaking.

"Petra, go inside," Abuelita said. "Now."

I shut my eyes and squeezed Luisito tight. He screamed, pushing himself away from me.

A restless night followed, and the violent wind gusts that had sent everyone to seek shelter inside their tents brought me a recurring nightmare. In it, I found myself in a field of sunflowers. I looked for Amelia and Luisito to show them the beautiful field but I couldn't find them. I wandered until I came across an old hut, and behind it, Amelia and Luisito sat on the edge of an abandoned well. Their backs were to me, and their feet dangled inside the deep, dark void. I froze at the sight. I was afraid to call out their names, afraid to move. I feared that my own breath would startle them and send them to their deaths. Next thing I knew, my belly was pressed against the ground and my arms stretched into the well. Amelia and Luisito desperately grasped at my hands and swung above the darkness, their eyes full of terror. Suddenly, their hands became damp and slipped through my fingers into the abyss.

I shook myself awake.

Immediately, I looked over at my siblings. Their gentle breathing let me know they slept soundly, but my heart wouldn't stop racing, and the feeling of helplessness still gripped me. I lay back down, afraid of closing my eyes and reliving the dream, afraid of not doing the right thing once the sun came up, afraid of failing to keep my promise to Papa.

I turned to my side and saw Abuelita sleeping. I wouldn't dare tell her of my bad dream. Otherwise, she'd try to convince me it was a sign. Abuelita's joints were aging, and our future was uncertain, and if she knew about my nightmare, it would probably sway her to give Luisito away.

seven

THE CONTRACT

Morning rays fell across the frosted ground. The storm from the night before had brought a northern gust that blew almost nonstop. People said these types of snap freezes, or *frío chiveros*, were rare this time of year. To mountain folk like us, this was not unusual, but without our serapes to shield us, we felt vulnerable.

A long row of tables had been assembled near the outskirts of the camp. Each table had a contractor sitting on one side and a line of anxious people ready to sign up for work on the other. Doña Juanita had stayed behind in our tent to care for Luisito, while Abuelita, Amelia, and I waited in one of the many lines.

This was our fifth line as the frigid wind whistled across the open field. The hope of securing a job kept us standing in the cold despite not being properly dressed for it. The four contactors we'd met earlier only hired men for mining, railroad work, and heavy labor. The line we stood in now, we were told, hired both men and women for farmwork.

The wind whipped my hair and made my body tense with cold. I wiggled my toes to keep them from growing numb as we waited in line. Amelia snuggled against Abuelita, who covered her with the end of her shawl. Not having a shawl of my own to keep me warm, I rubbed my bare arms frequently and bounced up and down on my toes to keep from shivering. I didn't want to appear weak in front of the contractors. I thought about the scorching desert we had crossed weeks earlier, which seemed to magically make me feel warmer.

After much waiting, the wind seemed to calm itself as we moved up the line and reached the contractor.

"*Cuántos años tener usted, señora?*" The contractor asked Abuelita. His Spanish was slow and sounded funny, almost as if his tongue had been caught in a snare. The man seemed to use his best Spanish, but still Abuelita gave him a confused look and turned to me.

"*Qué dice,* m'ija?" Abuelita said. "What's he saying?"

The past several days of picking up rations and seeing the camp doctors for vaccines and checkups had attuned my ears to accents and broken Spanish.

"He's asking your age," I said to Abuelita.

"I'm fifty-eight, *señor*," said Abuelita.

"And you?" The contractor glanced at me.

"I'm twelve," I said, straightening and raising my chin. "But I'll be thirteen soon."

The contractor used his pencil to point at Amelia and me. "Your *padres*, are they here, in the camp?"

"No, sir," I said. "It's only my grandmother, my sister, and my baby brother who stayed back in the tent."

The contactor put the pencil down, removed his hat, and rubbed his bald head. "Lo siento," the man apologized. "I can't hire you."

My shoulders dropped. "Why not?"

The contractor used the tip of his fingers to scratch above his eyebrows. "My agency has strict rules. If I hire people who can't fulfill their work, I lose my commission. I don't get paid."

I pressed my hands on the small table and leaned toward him. "I'm a hard worker. Back home I climbed trees—really tall trees—and chopped wood to sell."

"Field work is different," he said. "It's hard work."

Abuelita nodded. "It is, but señor, I assure you Petra can do it."

"I can, and besides," I said, "yesterday the man on the train said there was plenty of work for everyone. You're the fifth contractor we've seen, sir, and I really need the work."

The contractor tilted his head and shook it. "I wish I could tell you different, but I only hire men, boys, or complete families."

I looked at him puzzled. "Complete families?"

"I can't hire an old woman, a little girl, and a baby," said the contractor. "Out of four mouths to feed, you're the only one who can provide labor." The contractor turned to Amelia and pointed at her with his chin. "She might work, but not *mucho*."

My blood boiled with frustration.

Suddenly, the contactor sitting at the table next to us asked our contractor something in English. The other contractor was a thin, pale man with a long nose, and as he spoke, he glanced in my direction. The contractor in front of us asked him something, and both began a conversation I couldn't understand, but

I knew it was about me. At the end, the man in front of us threw his head back, laughing, and went on to shake his head. The skinny contractor smiled timidly and shrugged his shoulders as he mumbled words to himself.

"What is he saying?" I asked. "Is he offering work?"

"No," said the contractor, with his face still red. "He's asking about your scarf. He wants to know where you bought it. He said he's been searching for a purple scarf like yours for his niece for almost two months."

I reached up and touched my scarf. It was both soft and strong, which reminded me of Marietta, the captain of the Revolucionarios.

Amelia pulled away from Abuelita and spoke to the contractor in front of us. "Does his niece like the color purple like me?"

The contractor chuckled. "His niece likes white and purple, so he wants to surprise her with a white puppy wearing a purple scarf."

Amelia, Abuelita, and I looked baffled at each other. "Dogs wear scarfs in America?" Abuelita said under her breath.

The bald contractor kept talking. "But I told him

that instead of getting a purple scarf, he should dye the puppy purple just like his wife, who claims to be a natural blond yet dyes her hair yellow."

The more the man spoke, the more confused I became. Dogs wearing garments and people changing their hair color was beyond me. Perhaps something was getting lost in his broken Spanish.

The skinny contractor shouted in my direction. "*Cuánto?*" he asked, pointing at his neck.

Amelia glanced at me. "He wants to know how much your scarf costs?"

I nodded, and feeling flattered, I said, "No *la vendo*. It's a gift, *un regalo especial*."

The skinny man turned to our contractor for help understanding me, but the bald man turned to me instead as voices behind us asked in Spanish what the holdup was.

The contractor crossed his arms and turned back to me. "If you can't find work today, come back in three days. If I've met my quota by then..." His lips twitched. "Maybe I can hire you."

"Really?" I said, trying to grasp the sense of relief that seemed to run away. "You'll hire me?"

"I said *maybe. Quizás.*" The contractor straightened in his seat. "*No promesas.* Is that all right?"

I smiled and nodded. I had hoped to be hired, but this was a start.

eight

GONE

Three days had passed since our visit with the contractors. The air had warmed, and the number of refugees had shrunk by more than half. The camp buzzed with people saying farewell. Those who had decided to remain in America showed off their train tickets while those who had decided to return to Mexico scrambled to gather news about the revolution. Every face carried the same nervousness, as if storm clouds of an uncertain future brewed above us.

I picked up our rations in the early morning and helped Doña Juanita prepare our breakfast. For the past three days, we had not said much to each other. She hadn't brought up her desire to take Luisito back to Mexico, and I hadn't mentioned it either.

Doña Juanita glanced at me before her eyes turned back to the pot she stirred. "I'm sorry you didn't secure any work the other day," she said in a quiet voice.

I observed her quietly, looking at her face to see if her words had been sincere.

"What's your plan if you don't get any work?" she asked.

"I *am* getting work," I said. "After we eat, I'm visiting a contractor who told me he'd have work for me."

"*Que bien.*" Doña Juanita smiled. "That's wonderful."

"It is," I said, "because once I'm hired, I'll get train tickets and a job that'll let me take care of Abuelita, Amelia, *and* Luisito."

Doña Juanita's smile faded, and she remained quiet as she stirred. After a moment she stopped and turned me. "I spoke to your grandmother about Luisito."

My hands tightened into fists. Abuelita hadn't mentioned anything.

"It was this morning," she said, "while you were getting the rations." Her eyes went back to the pot. "I truly want what's best for Luisito," she said in a calm voice, "and I was out of place when I asked to take him."

I wondered if she really meant what she'd said and waited for her to say more.

"I've come to realize that what's important for Luisito is for him to be with you—his family."

I felt a flood of relief, but I'd never seen Doña Juanita this sad. A bitter taste formed in my mouth, and when I swallowed, it turned into a hard little ball on my chest. I thought about how much Doña Juanita had done for Luisito and how I had treated her.

"I know you love Luisito as much as we do," I said.

Doña Juanita gave a sad smile and nodded with her eyes still on the pot.

"I met a man yesterday who recently arrived from Guanajuato," she said. "According to him, it's all a disaster." Doña Juanita sniffled and cleared her throat. "He claimed that every town he passed had been nearly destroyed."

"Don't go back," I said to Doña Juanita. "Come with us instead."

Doña Juanita forced a smile. "Petra, I can't. My mother, she's blind and feeble, and I know she had to stay behind. I need to go back and make sure she's well."

"Can you go back later, once it's safe?" I asked.

Doña Juanita shook her head. "I wanted to get back to her before, but I had a son to protect. On my way here, the desert took him and my husband away, and now without them, I feel I have nothing to lose by going back."

A tear snuck out of Doña Juanita's eye, but she swiftly wiped it away. "I also feel an obligation to Mexico. It's my country, my homeland. If the Federales are close to being defeated like the man said, I want to be there to help rebuild her."

I understood. I too had the urge to help my country and an urge to go find Papa, but keeping my promise to him, to take care of our family, weighed heavier.

Doña Juanita looked defeated, but still she smiled. "I'll stay in the camp until you get hired," she said. "I want to make sure you're all fine until you board the train."

"Thank you," I said, dreading the day we had to part. It was going to be painful for everyone, especially for Luisito.

After we had our breakfast, Amelia and I rushed out of the tent and headed to see the contractor.

"Why didn't we go see the contractor yesterday?" asked Amelia as we ran down the aisles among the tents.

"Because he told us to see him in three days," I said, holding Amelia's hand.

"But yesterday was three days."

"No," I said. "Today makes three days." I used my fingers to recount the days as a sick feeling came to me. After a moment of doubt, I convinced myself I had it right.

My heart raced as we walked past the last block of tents, and when we rounded the final tent, I came to a complete stop.

"What's wrong?" asked Amelia.

I didn't answer. My mind scrambled, counting the days since I'd last seen the bald contractor, trying to figure out what had happened. The long row of tables was gone, and only one lonely table stood in its place.

I let go of Amelia's hand and ran toward the lone contactor sitting at the table. I cut in front of the line, and a wave of shouts and hissing sounds came from behind me.

"*Dónde están todos?* Where's everybody?" I asked the contractor, catching my breath. I realized it was the same skinny, long-nosed contractor who had asked about my purple scarf.

"*Todos?*" he said, looking around him. "*Contratistas?*"

"Yes, the contractors. Where are they?" I asked.

The man raised his shoulders. "Gone," he said. "*Contratistas no aquí. Solo yo.*"

He smiled at me and then motioned the man behind me to step up.

I shoved myself in front of the man. "How about the contractor that sat next to you? The bald one?" I pointed to my hair and tried to speak like him. "*Contratista no pelo?*"

The man chuckled, and his eyes widened like he had understood me. "*Contratista a casa, no aquí. Contratista lejos.*" He then said something in English that made his eyes tell me that the contractor was long gone and that he felt sorry.

A voice behind me spoke. "*Con permiso, niña.*" It was the man I had blocked from the contractor. He nodded before going around me.

I stepped aside slowly, feeling dizzy and nauseous at the sounds of the camp coming down. Tarps flapped in the air, and American soldiers hammered out iron spikes that held down each tent and threw them into crates. Their voices shouted words in English to each other as crates were quickly loaded into wagons.

Amelia pulled at my arm. "Did you get the job? Did he give you the train tickets?"

I looked at her. She shaded her eyes, but despite their squint, I could see a sparkle of hope in them as she waited for my answer. I could feel my shoulders grow heavy.

"No," I mumbled.

American soldiers hustled to bring down the camp while the rest of the people hurried with their belongings. Some headed toward the bridge, back to Mexico, to try and find their old lives, and others toward the train to start a new ones. We only had three more days left in the camp. If I didn't find work, my family and I would be deported. We'd be forced to walk across the bridge, forced to face the war and hunger all over again.

nine

THE DEAL

In the days that followed, I'd made several trips to the open field searching for the bald contractor, but hadn't found him.

On the third day, the day the camp was to be closed, I woke with a heart so heavy, it was hard to breathe. Still, I made myself look for the contractor one last time but only saw the same long-nosed, skinny man. He waved happily at me, and I waved back before turning to pick up our last rations.

The big crowd that had dominated every morning had dwindled to a few scattered souls. There were so few of us, we were no longer required to form a line. From atop a boxcar, a single American soldier placed the rations into the baskets. I walked up to the small crowd and waited my turn.

My eyes diverted to a girl next to me. She was about my height and my age with eyes greener than a fresh cactus pad. Their color stood out beautifully against her dark skin. She was barefoot too, though her clothes were not as ragged as mine. I'd never seen her before.

She caught me looking at her, and I quickly turned my eyes away. I didn't feel like talking to anyone, but something inside me pushed me to talk to her. Maybe it was because she looked just as nervous as I felt, or maybe because I thought I could make her feel better.

"*Buenos días,*" I said sheepishly.

The girl returned the greeting with a nervous smile.

"Is this your last day here too?" I asked.

She nodded, glancing around. More than half of the camp's tents and woodstoves had been disassembled.

"I think it's everybody's last day here," she said.

Her comment made me chuckle. "I meant if it's your last day in America?"

"Oh," she said, her face blushing. "No—well, yes. I think we're going back."

The girl's answer confused me. We continued to take small steps toward the boxcar as the crowd moved up.

"You didn't get a job with one of the contractors?" I asked.

The girl shook her head. "I didn't, but my papa got hired yesterday. He signed the contract, got the tickets, but now he's having second thoughts about staying."

I gave her a baffled look. "Why?"

"He wants to go back to my mother. She's with child."

"Why didn't she come with you?"

"The baby in my mother's belly made her very sick and weak, and when she could no longer care for my brothers and me, she sent us all to live with my tía, near the border. My papa promised to leave us there and head back to her, but the revolution came and pushed us all the way across the border."

"Do you know if your mama is okay?"

"We know she's due in a couple of weeks, but we have no idea how she's doing."

My heart ached for her. I remembered Mama and how weak she had become after delivering Luisito. She looked so pale holding him and quickly left this world after a few days.

"Yesterday," the girl continued, "after accepting a job, my father said he would take us to a place called San Antonio. He said he would settle us there and then go back for my mother. But this morning he had a change of heart and said we'd all go back instead."

"Do you want to go back?" I asked.

"I do because I want to see my mama, but at the same time, I'm scared of the revolution."

"I heard it's getting better," I said, hoping my words would comfort her.

The girl straightened her shoulders a bit. "My papa heard that too. That's why we're saving these last rations for the trip back."

"Maybe your papa can use the tickets later once you know your mama is fine."

The girl shook her head as the American soldier poured corn, beans, and flour into her baskets. "The tickets are only good for today." The girl gave the soldier a quick glance then turned to me and whispered, "My papa is trying to sell all four tickets, but he's having trouble finding someone to buy them."

The girl thanked the American soldier, and a thought flashed through my mind.

"Suerte." The girl wished me luck and struggled to balance the heavy baskets as she turned to walk away.

"Wait!" I said to her, and she halted. I looked up at the American soldier, rushing him with my gaze.

"The tickets," I said, grabbing my filled baskets and catching up with her. "How much is your papa selling them for?"

"I don't know."

"I'll buy them," I said.

The girl gave me strange look but then nodded and smiled. "Go drop off your rations first then meet me here. Our tent is on the other end of the—"

"No," I said, afraid the ticket would be sold before I even got to my tent. "I'll follow you now."

My arms struggled to carry the heavy baskets as I tried keeping up with the girl's long strides. My mind churned. I had no money. I'd have to think of something to offer soon.

"*Papá*," said the girl as we neared the tent.

A man, who appeared much older than Papa, came out. His skin looked like leather, as if he'd spent many hours under the desert sun.

He approached his daughter, taking the baskets.

"Papá, this is..." The girl turned to me.

"Petra Luna, señor," I said, putting my baskets on the ground.

The man bowed his head, acknowledging my introduction.

"Petra wants to know how much you're selling the tickets for," the girl said.

"I have one person interested already but says he has no money. He said he'd go out and find some."

"I'll buy them," I said.

The man took a step closer to me. "*Cuánto tienes?* How much do you have?"

My eyes darted around me until they fell on my overflowing baskets. "I'll give you all my rations for the tickets."

"All your rations?" said the man. "Have you asked your parents?"

The girl spoke for me. "It's only her grandmother and siblings who are here with her."

"Maybe you should ask your *abuela* first," said the man. "Besides, those rations are only worth about half of what I'm asking for."

"Please, señor," I said. "Take these for now. I promise I'll come back with more."

"More rations?" the man said. "I already have plenty of food. What I need now is money."

"Papá," said the girl. "We can always sell the food too." She turned back to me with a clever grin.

The man sighed and stared at his daughter.

"*Órale, pues*," said the man. "I'll take these rations, but the rest I'll need in cash. Get me at least fifty American centavos and the passes are yours. And make it quick because the train leaves in about an hour."

"I'll get the money for you, señor, just please don't sell the tickets to anyone."

"He won't," said the girl. Her father chuckled and shook his head.

I gave them both a wide smile and took off running toward my tent.

"Where are the rations?" asked Abuelita.

"I gave them away," I said, catching my breath. "To a man who's selling train tickets."

"Where are the tickets?" asked Doña Juanita, carrying Luisito.

"I don't have them yet," I said.

"You gave him the food without getting the train tickets?" asked Abuelita. "He's probably gone by now."

"No," I said. "He's waiting for me to get the money I owe him." My eyes looked around inside our tent to see what else I could come up with or sell.

"How much money?" asked Doña Juanita.

"Fifty American cents," I said.

Abuelita looked shocked. "*Quién se cree ese hombre?* Who does he think he is, selling those passes?"

"It doesn't matter," I said. "He's selling four tickets, and I need to buy them."

"Can we give him my rations?" asked Doña Juanita.

"No," said Abuelita. "Those are yours. You'll need that food in Mexico, just like we'll need ours when we get sent back tomorrow." She glared at me.

"The man said he's already got enough food," I said and rubbed the top of my head and then my neck, nervous that I couldn't find anything. "What he needs now is money."

Suddenly, with my hand on the back of my neck, I'd found something I could sell.

"What?" asked Amelia when I stopped moving.

"I could sell my scarf," I said.

"No," Amelia said with wide eyes. "That's special to you. It was a gift."

Amelia was right. It was special. It'd been given to me by one of the bravest women I'd known. Part of me wanted to shut the idea out of my mind, but selling the purple scarf was probably the only way to keep us from going back to Mexico. I made up my mind, and as close as I felt to Marietta with this scarf and as strong and brave as I believed to be when I wore it, it was something I'd have to let go of.

ten

FIFTY CENTS

I marched out of the tent, knowing exactly who I was going to sell my scarf to.

Amelia tried to keep up with me. "You can't sell it, Petra." Her voice almost broke as she spoke. "The scarf is special to you."

"We'll be fine," I said.

Amelia and I reached the open field, and the contractor sat alone at the table, looking down at a stack of papers he held. Since there was no line waiting for him, I walked straight to the table. He glanced up at me, squinting in the morning sun.

"Buenos días," he said.

I smiled and untied my scarf and let its softness fall through my fingers one last time. I placed it on the table

but before I could speak, Amelia said "*Sesenta* centavos."
I turned to Amelia, and she wrinkled her nose at me.

"*Setenta?*" said the contactor, misunderstanding that
Amelia had said sixty.

"*Sí,*" Amelia said with excitement and raised seven
fingers. "Setenta. Seventy!"

"Oh, no, setenta—*mucho dinero,*" said the contractor.

"*Bueno,* sesenta." Amelia raised six fingers this time.
The man rubbed his chin.

"*Mire.*" Amelia picked the scarf up, bringing it closer
to the man. "*Está muy bonita y muy suavecita.*"

"*Sí,*" said the man. "Muy bonita." He cocked his head
to the side and gave Amelia a grin. "*Cincuenta,*" he said,
holding five fingers up.

"No." Amelia shook her head repeatedly and raised
six fingers again. "*Sesenta.*"

The man sucked in his breath, and his smile started
to fade.

"Cincuenta!" I shouted and pushed the scarf toward
him.

The man pursed his lips then smiled and nodded. He
reached for his pocket, and into my hand, he dropped
five small silver coins.

I thanked the man and walked away, glancing back at the scarf for the very last time and remembering Marietta. My neck felt shivery and exposed without it.

"Why did you interrupt me?" said Amelia as we headed to get the train passes.

"Because he was about to back out," I said, "and the train is leaving in thirty minutes. We don't have much time."

"We were so close to getting more."

"It doesn't matter," I said. "We're leaving soon."

The girl with the green eyes sat outside her tent. "Did you get the money?" she shouted.

"I did," I said. Her father came out of the tent carrying four yellow strips of paper.

"Here you go, señor." I handed him the coins, one by one, counting in tens. Each coin had what appeared to be the profile of an Apache on one side and a buffalo on the other. "Cincuenta centavos," I said at the end.

The man picked up one of the coins and said, "*Estos son nicles, no son daimes.*"

I looked at him, confused.

"Each of these coins is only worth five cents," he said. "This is only twenty-five cents."

My heart sank. "I think I...or maybe the gringo..."

"It doesn't matter, m'ija," said the man. "This is a lot more than I could have hoped for, and the train is about to leave. Here are the tickets."

I took the yellow strips of paper and instinctively threw my arms around him. "*Gracias*, señor."

Amelia and I were rushing to our tent when she suddenly stopped. "I have to say bye to my friend and her rooster. Can I go quick?"

"We have to make it quick because I still have to help Abuelita pack our things."

"I can go by myself," said Amelia. "You go on, and I'll catch up in a bit."

"Don't take too long," I shouted as Amelia disappeared around a tent.

The soldiers continued to clear the camp, hauling away disassembled tents, corn grinders, and bricks used in the outdoor woodstoves.

"These passes will take us all the way to San Antonio," I said as we all rushed to pack the food and blankets we'd been given.

"Where's San Antonio?" asked Doña Juanita.

"The man told me it was a big city up north, not far

from here," I said. "He also said there was a lot of work there."

The train's horn whistled, announcing its arrival. It would only be minutes before everyone would board the train and leave.

"Where's Amelia?" asked Abuelita.

"Meh-mia?" asked Luisito.

I tightened everything in a bundle, using Abuelita's shawl. "She went to say bye to her friend," I said. "But she said it wouldn't take her long."

We stepped out of the tent and couldn't see Amelia.

"Start walking to the train," I said. "I'll go search for her."

Doña Juanita, carrying Luisito, headed toward the train.

"Give me the bundle," said Abuelita. "You need to run and find Amelia, otherwise we'll miss the train."

I handed Abuelita the bundle and ran down the scattered rows of tents left standing. Amelia was nowhere to be found. I went back down each row, and this time I began calling out for her.

"Amelia," I shouted, becoming more agitated. Again, I couldn't find her and, looking at the river, I wondered if she'd gone there to find her friend. I dashed to the river, calling for her.

The train's horn whistle made me run faster, and when I heard my name coming from behind me, I stopped. It was Amelia. She stood near the last row of tents.

"Where were you?" I yelled at her. "Everyone's at the train already. What took you so long?"

Amelia's face was red, and she seemed to be out of breath, but still she managed to say, "I'll race you to the train."

Even at six years old, Amelia could outrun me.

A small crowd had gathered around the train, and one man, dressed like us, argued with another man who appeared to be in charge. He wore spectacles and a black uniform with shiny buttons that matched the brass letter on his cap. The man with the ragged clothes insisted on boarding with his chickens and goat while the uniformed man told him things were different in America. Animals weren't allowed on trains.

As we all said our goodbyes, Abuelita wiped her tears and Amelia sobbed. Doña Juanita kissed Luisito one last time and let him wrap his arms tight around her neck. I could see Doña Juanita holding back tears as she patted Luisito's back and whispered into his ear.

Finally, when the time came to board, I helped Abuelita pull Luisito away from Doña Juanita. He twisted like a worm and wailed almost as loud as the train's whistle. Luisito was only about a year old, but somehow he seemed to know this was the last time we'd see Doña Juanita.

I hugged Doña Juanita again and thanked her for being so good to us. Within moments, Amelia and Abuelita and I waved at her from our window, and Luisito stuck his hand out as if hoping to touch her one last time.

Doña Juanita reached for Luisito's hand and kissed it. She held it until the train's brass bell clanged and the train began to pull away.

Luisito's wailing caught the attention of the same uniformed man we'd seen earlier. He stood in the aisle not far from us, collecting train passes. He inspected every pass and used a small gadget he carried to punch a hole in each one. Then he'd slip the tickets into little frames above each row of seats. His face was stern, and as he inched his way toward us, Luisito's cries made him glance at us between ticket inspections.

Thankfully, Luisito's fussing had turned into a soft whimper by the time the man reached our row.

The man took his time examining each of our tickets front and back, over and over again. His silence made me uncomfortable. What if the tickets weren't valid? If so, we'd probably be kicked off the train, thrown in prison for theft, or worse yet, be sent back to Mexico.

The man finally put the tickets together and tapped them against his palm. He drew in a breath, looked at the back door, and then turned back at us silently, as if contemplating what to do next. After what seemed like forever, he looked at me over his spectacles, cleared his throat, and spoke. "You don't belong here."

eleven

CRYSTALS AND VELVET

My face burned. I could hardly move, and after swallowing hard, I forced myself to speak. "Where do we belong?"

The man pointed down the aisle toward the back door.

I stretched my neck and turned back to see the door. "Outside? You...you mean we belong off the train?"

The man chuckled and shook his head. "These tickets are first class."

"First class?" I said, making sure I had understood his Spanish, which seemed better than everyone else's.

Nodding, the man slipped the tickets into his silver gadget and squeezed.

"Here." The man returned the tickets with a hole

punched through them. "Count five cars down that way. Once you've entered the first-class car, pick a seat, then place the tickets inside a metal frame like this one." He tapped on the frame above the outer seat then continued his way down the aisle.

I turned to Abuelita, "What's first class?"

Abuelita shrugged "*No se*, m'ija, but it sounds fancy."

"Whatever it is," I said, "it's better than getting kicked off the train."

Amelia jumped off her seat and rushed to the back door, ahead of us.

With my hands still shaking, I handed our belongings to Abuelita and carried Luisito all the way to first class.

Amelia held the door open for us. "This is the one. I counted five cars like the man said."

I stepped into the car, and instinctively my toes curled, hugging the softness beneath them. I paused and glanced down. Under my feet was a thick fabric of colorful threads woven into different patterns. I took slow steps and observed the marvels around me—velvet curtains, shiny brass, and wood so polished, you could see yourself in it. It was as if I had entered a small palace.

The car was nearly empty except for an Anglo couple who sat near the entrance and a man sitting behind them, reading a newspaper. The woman gave a surprised look when she first saw me, and after whispering something to the man next to her, her expression softened.

Abuelita pointed out two empty rows that faced each other near the center, and as we passed the Anglo couple, the woman smiled and waved at Luisito.

We all sat on green plush seats that were as thick as a block of cheese.

Abuelita smiled nervously. "This is what angels must feel when they sit on clouds."

I noticed the shiny rack above us and set our food bundle on it. Amelia, who'd snuck away for a moment, surprised us with a crystal glass full of icy water. We all took turns sipping from it and wondered how Americans could get water to be so cold this time of year.

An hour into our ride, Luisito fell asleep on Abuelita's lap. I sat across from them by the window and thought Amelia was asleep with her head fixed on my shoulder until a tall, slender man carrying a large tray strapped to his shoulders entered the car.

Amelia sprang up. "Is that man selling tacos?"

"I can't smell them," said Abuelita. "I don't think they're tacos."

The man approached our row, and what he said in English was probably an offer of what laid on his tray. They weren't tacos. They were small triangles of sliced bread, overlapping each other like fallen dominos, and in between every two slices was a thin line of something brown and red that looked mushy. The whole thing looked cold and unappetizing.

Without an expression, the man stared at me, waiting for our response. I smiled and after I shook my head, the man continued down the aisle.

"What were those?" asked Amelia. "They looked good."

"You'd eat that stuff?" I said, wrinkling my nose.

Amelia nodded repeatedly and pointed at our stash above. "You think I can trade something for a little triangle?"

"No," said Abuelita. "Remember what that man said earlier? Things are different in America." Abuelita then looked to the side before leaning toward us. "Have you noticed that people here even laugh differently?" Abuelita used her eyes to point at the Anglo couple across the aisle.

"I like different," said Amelia, looking back at the man with the tray.

A little later, after Abuelita had leaned her head back to sleep, Amelia whispered to me. "Petra."

I turned to Amelia, and her eyes dropped to her clasped hands resting over her lap.

"I have something for you," she said in a low voice.

"What is it?" I asked.

Amelia gave a quick glance to Abuelita, who still had her eyes shut. When Amelia opened her hands, my jaw nearly hit the floor.

"Amelia," I gasped. My purple scarf was scrunched up between her hands.

Amelia looked up at me with a smile. "I told you I was fast."

"How—" I said. "Did you steal it from him?"

"I didn't," said Amelia. "He left it on the table. He didn't care about it."

"How do you know that? Maybe he was going to the outhouse."

"If he really cared, he would've taken it with him to the outhouse."

"Amelia, you shouldn't have done that," I said.

"Well, he shouldn't have given you half the money you asked for."

"That still doesn't make it right, and you know that," I said. "Maybe he misunderstood us and thought we meant five coins."

Amelia frowned and looked down at the scarf. "I know it wasn't right, but I know how much this scarf means to you. I didn't want some dog wearing it when it's so important to you."

I chuckled. "So that's why your face was so red? That's why you asked me to race you to the train?"

Amelia nodded with a mischievous smile. "I didn't know how long he'd be gone."

I took the scarf from Amelia's hands. It felt good to feel its softness once again. I turned and gave her a big squeeze. "Thank you," I said and kissed the top of her head.

"Can I help you tie it back around your neck?"

"Sure," I said.

Amelia's eyes gleamed after knotting the scarf. "There," she said.

Moments later, after she fell asleep on my lap, I could still see the proud smile on her lips.

I leaned my head against the window and looked outside. The train sped faster than anything I'd ever seen, and by now my world was changing in every direction. Outside, the trees were getting fuller and the open fields greener. The desert, the mountains, and the canyons had been replaced by flat grasslands. There were no more makeshift graves or burned-down homes scattered about. We were entering a whole new world.

twelve

A NEW WORLD

Distant sounds of metal clanging, wheels squeaking, and the blasting horn of the train awoke me. I sprung up in my seat and looked around me then outside.

"Petra." Abuelita grabbed my arm. "Are you all right, m'ija?"

I took in a deep breath and nodded. "How long was I asleep?"

Abuelita leaned back on her seat. "About two hours."

Amelia sat by the window, carrying Luisito on her lap. She pointed at different things we passed. "You see that pretty tree, Luisito? Look at those horses."

Luisito slapped the window with his palms and spat on it as he blabbered on and on. The window was far from being crystal clear like it'd been before the trip.

My body swayed gently with the train's motion, and I felt safe, almost like a baby being rocked in its mother's arms.

I began to wonder how much longer we had left when the same uniformed man from the start of our trip entered our car. In strange-sounding Spanish, he shouted, "San Antonio! San Antonio!" and walked down the aisle before disappearing through the back door.

Abuelita smiled and pointed outside, where the city was beginning to take shape. Wooden homes, like the ones near the refugee camp, and huts like the ones from Mexico lined the tracks. The buildings grew taller and bigger, and before long, the train chugged to a stop, releasing a long hiss at the end.

Not far from our window stood an ivory building with bell towers at its corners and a tall dome in the center. The building reminded me of the church we'd stayed in during our escape from the Federales in Mexico, but the large stained-glass windows didn't display saints or crosses. They displayed symbols I'd never seen before.

"Look, Abuelita," said Amelia. "A church. Maybe they have *pan pobre* there."

Abuelita leaned toward the window, and together we

observed the crowds entering and exiting the building through its wide arched doors.

We stepped off the train, and ribbons of white steam swirled around our feet. The air was filled with all sorts of noises—trains hooting, bells ringing, people shouting. We inched our way through the confusion as the smell of burnt oil and smoke stung my nose. Streams of people walked past us with purpose—workers wearing blue overalls, women in fancy dresses, and men dressed like the contractors in the camp.

"Can we take a peek inside the church?" said Amelia.

"I don't think it's a church," I said and pointed at the bronze figure atop the dome. "There's no cross up there."

Amelia stood still and narrowed her eyes on the figure.

"It's an Apache!" she said. "What's he aiming at with his bow?"

I was about to shrug when I paused and noticed the sunset's orange glow fall over the Apache's back. "The sunrise," I said, my heart pounding. "He's aiming at the start of a new day. Kind of like—"

"It's a train station," said Abuelita. "You see the people walking in and out with suitcases?"

Our attention turned to Luisito the moment he began fussing.

"I think he's tired," said Abuelita, handing Luisito to me.

"I thought he slept the whole way," I said.

"No, he woke up soon after you and Amelia fell asleep," said Abuelita. "Where do we go now?"

"I don't know," I said. "Let's keep walking and see what we come across."

"What if we can't find a place to sleep?" asked Amelia.

"That's the least of our worries," said Abuelita. "We've always found a place to sleep. Besides, we're in San Antonio." She looked up at the sky and crossed herself. "Saint Anthony is the patron saint of lost possessions. We'll find a place in no time."

We followed the crowd and walked down a busy street toward what appeared to be the center of town. On the sidewalks, people greeted each other, gave directions, and talked about the revolution in Mexico—all in Spanish. Their voices mingled with those coming from the busy shops and saloons.

Everyone I saw was brown like me and spoke like me. Even the vendors were Mexican. They chanted about their goods in Spanish and sold everything from round pecan candies to meat snacks with pepper sauce. Their cries carried a tune, meant to sway people into buying their goods. My stomach rumbled as each vendor described the food with their chant.

Beggars were scattered along the sidewalks. Their ragged, filthy clothes made them look like scarecrows. There were also women with distant, blank faces who, by the number of small children clinging to them, appeared to have too many mouths to feed. I stared and wondered about their dreary lives. Perhaps this place didn't have enough work for everyone.

"Petra," said Abuelita with a heavy sigh. "My knees are killing me. I need to sit."

I led Abuelita to an iron bench a few steps away from what seemed to be an open market. After she sat, I placed Luisito and our bundle next to her and glanced at a man sitting at the opposite end of the bench. He wore simple but well-kept clothes and leaned over a small wooden table in front of him.

He was an *escribano*, a penman, who was writing a letter for a customer standing nearby. The customer was a tall man with a thick mustache and ragged clothes. He held his tattered straw hat over his chest as he told the penman what to write on the paper.

Quiet as could be, I walked over and leaned to see how the escribano wrote. I let my eyes follow his pen as it waltzed across the paper, decorating each letter with smooth curves and fancy hooks.

The escribano dipped the pen into the ink bottle and offered it to his customer. "*Firme aquí*," he said and pointed to the bottom of the letter. "Sign here."

The man took the pen and marked a cross at the bottom of the paper. He knew how to write as much as I did.

"Petra," Abuelita called. "Amelia walked around the corner a while ago and hasn't come back." She looked nervous as she glanced at the busy streets and the large crowds flowing in and out of the open market. We'd seen this many people at the refugee camp, but things here seemed to move faster and louder.

"Come, Luisito," I said, scooping up my brother. "We better find Amelia."

thirteen
THE WESLEY HOUSE

I carried Luisito and walked through the crowds for a block before I spotted Amelia. She stood talking to a woman who sat on the ground with a steaming pot—a food vendor. I couldn't hear them, but Amelia motioned her arms and bounced up and down as if playing out a story. The woman had a rounded, hunched back and appeared to be entertained as she stirred the pot. Nearby, on a little stove, were at least a dozen tortillas spread across a scorched tin sheet.

"Amelia," I said. "What are you doing?"

Amelia turned to me, holding a taco in each hand. She tilted her head toward me. "This is my sister," Amelia said to the hunchbacked woman.

I introduced myself and turned back to Amelia. "Give the food back."

"But it's for you and Abuelita," said Amelia.

"Amelia, you know we have no money," I said. "Give it back."

"M'ija," said the woman. She sunk her hand into a pail behind her and lifted a handful of cooked corn from the yellowish water. "Your sister told me all about your journey. Please, take the food." She placed the corn on a metate and began crushing it.

As hungry as I was and as tasty as the food smelled, I shook my head. "I'm sorry, but—"

"But nothing," said the hunched back woman. "People from *el macizo*, the solid Mexican homeland, help each other." She paused and used her forearm to wipe the sweat off her forehead. "Once you get your life together, you too will be able to help others."

I wanted to believe the hunchbacked woman, but with as much help as my family and I needed in this new place, being able to help others seemed far-fetched. I took a deep breath and looked at everything—the shops, the vendors, the beggars, the women with blue shawls draped over their shoulders, and the men with the wide-brimmed sombreros—everything was the same as it had been back home before the war. Even the language was the same.

"America looks just like Mexico," I said to her.

The hunchbacked woman chuckled as she handed me a taco. "It looks the same because you're in the west side—*Los Corrales*—or what some people call Little Mexico. You won't see too many gringos, *negros*, or *chinos* around here. Only brown faces like ours."

Amelia finished eating one of the tacos in her hands then dashed back up the street to give the other to Abuelita. I sat Luisito on the ground next to me and took the taco the woman offered.

"How long have you lived here?" I asked.

"About seven months," she said. Just then two men stopped to buy tacos from the woman. As I waited for her to serve the customers, I tore off a small piece of totilla from my taco and gave it to Luisito.

"I like it here," the woman said after the men had left. "You see these?" She lifted her cupped hand, showing me the coins they had paid her.

I nodded.

"This here is opportunity," she said, "and opportunities are everywhere in America." She placed the coins inside the pocket on her apron and went back to grinding the corn. "But opportunities don't fall from the sky like rain," the hunchbacked woman said. "They only come to you when you work hard."

I bit into my taco, savoring the spiced potatoes and onions with a touch of roasted beef. I glanced across the street at a park where a gazebo stood surrounded by tall trees and flowery bushes. Past the park stood an enormous building. It had five levels and appeared to occupy the entire block. It was the biggest building I'd ever seen.

I pointed to it. "Is that the town's palace over there?"

The woman turned back. "That's the Santa Rosa. It's an infirmary ran by nuns and doctors. A hospital."

In Mexico, while at a rebel camp, we'd taken Luisito to a hospital train because he'd been sick. I remembered its clean smell, its white walls, and the friendly doctor who helped make Luisito feel better. This enormous building was at least a hundred times bigger than the hospital train, and I couldn't imagine what a building that size could do for the sick.

"Petra," Amelia shouted, running to us. "Abuelita is really tired. She said her bones hurt a lot."

"You all should go to *la casa Wesley*," the woman said.

"You can rest there for the night." She stood, wiped her hands across her apron, and pointed at the street near us. "Walk six blocks south, that way, until you see a yellow two-story house surrounded by an iron fence. It'll have a big sign hanging over the entrance that reads *Wesley House*."

"Who's Wesley?" I said.

The woman shrugged. "*Sepa la bola*. All I know is that the house is run by nuns who help people like us."

It didn't take long before we reached the yellow house with the iron fence. I saw the sign hanging above like the hunchbacked woman had mentioned, but I couldn't read what it said. Above us, early stars had begun to twinkle, but from inside the house, light shined so bright, you'd swear that Huitzilopochtli, the Aztec god of the sun, lived there.

The nuns inside the Wesley House spoke Spanish that I half understood, but their smiles were as warm and welcoming as the soup they offered us.

The house was crowded with people like us who

had just arrived from Mexico or from refugee camps. Despite how busy the nuns were, they gave Abuelita a special tea to ease her pain. They also gave us a white powder for Luisito that, when mixed with water, tasted almost like milk. We were given clean clothes, shoes, and blankets for the night.

After we ate our soup, one of the nuns took us down the hall to a tiny room near the back of the house.

"This is a toilet," said the nun, pointing at a white porcelain bowl the size of a chair. The bowl had a wooden lid with a big hole in the center. Inside the bowl, at the bottom, was a small pool of water, and up high on the wall was a large porcelain box with a long chain.

The nun continued, "After you're done using it, pull on the chain like this to make everything go away." She showed us, and Amelia jumped back as water gushed into the bowl, swirled in circles, and made loud gargling sounds. Right before our eyes, all the water disappeared through the bottom.

Amelia gasped as she peeked from my side. "Can you do that again?" She asked the nun, and for the rest of the evening, Amelia found any excuse to use the toilet and watch it flush.

Another room nearby had a large white tub—large enough to fit a grown man. A metal pipe stuck up from the floor and bent high above the tub, holding a thick metal plate with rows of holes in it.

Shivering and undressed, Amelia, Luisito, and I stood inside the tub, under the plate. But no sooner had I pulled on a lever than a stream of water shot out of each hole. It was like summer rain, each droplet warm and soft against our skin.

Amelia and Luisito jumped and splashed in the water, and in between their laughter, I could hear Mama laughing too. I shut my eyes for a moment and in my mind saw Mama laughing as she held Amelia and me by the hand and danced in the rain with us.

At the end of the day, we all lay on thick blankets spread across the wooden floor. Soon everyone was asleep, except for me.

In the darkness, I could make out the glass bulb hanging from the ceiling. It was now turned off, but my amazement hadn't ceased. How could light as bright as the sun be captured in such a small thing?

America was a place filled with so many wonders— icy water, flushing toilets, showers, and daylight at night. My day had started with me not knowing if I was going to stay in America, and now I lay here on the most beautiful floor I'd ever seen.

I reached for my black rock and brought it to my chest, holding it with both hands. If the hunchbacked woman was right about the many opportunities here, I was going to work hard to keep my family safe, learn to read and write, and find ways to bring Papa back into our lives. My thoughts went to the Apache figure atop the train station. Like him, I wanted to aim and hurl my arrows at every rising opportunity. And the sooner I learned how and where to aim my bow and arrow, the quicker I could make my dreams come true.

fourteen

THE WASP'S NEST

Before the sun came up, morning fog hung low over the street and wrapped around the bushes outside the Wesley House. It added to the mystery of this new place, and unlike the noisy night before, the house was quiet with everyone sleeping.

I looked out a large window and sat in comfort and warmth near the kitchen's kerosene stove. In front of me was a steaming bowl of something I'd never seen before. It was thick and creamy with a hint of sweetness. It reminded me of *atole*, a drink we made during holidays, except the aroma of toasted cornmeal was missing. I soon learned it was called oatmeal.

Despite the fog, the food, and the excitement of a new city, I was preoccupied with the brown leather shoes on my feet. The nuns had given them to me and advised me to wear them when I went searching for work. They claimed wearing shoes would help me secure a job. Still, I didn't like them. They felt like stones over my feet—heavy, cold, and suffocating.

"Find a place to live first," said one of the nuns to me as I ate breakfast. "You can look for work later." She began giving me directions to different neighborhoods.

"I'm sorry," I said, interrupting her. "We have no money at all. Shouldn't I get a job first?"

The nun shook her head. "The city is flooded with refugees. It gets tougher every day to find a place. Find a home first and a job later." She mentioned three places nearby where we might find a home.

"If they ask for a deposit, tell them that the Wesley House sent you," said the nun. "Many times, they'll waive the deposit charge."

As I got ready to leave, Abuelita stepped into the kitchen.

"M'ija," said Abuelita. "Are you leaving already?"

"I am," I said and bowed my head to get her blessings. After Abuelita made the sign of the cross over me, she stepped back. "You seem taller."

I pulled my skirt up and showed off my laced-up shoes. "They're not comfortable, but the nuns said they'll help me find work. How are you feeling today?"

"I feel better," said Abuelita. "Go on, m'ija. *Ve con Dios.* I'll see you at noon."

With a stomach full of knots, I walked out of the house. I couldn't speak the language in this new land, nor read or write, but I found strength when I reached into my pocket and squeezed my baby diamond. I had to be brave like Papa. I had to be brave for my family and for my promise to him.

I shut the iron gate behind me, and in the light of day, I looked up at the Wesley House. The roof of the house was different from the flat roofs in Mexico. This roof was angled and seemed to be sagging at the corners. With the yellow peeling walls and the dark patches scattered across the roof, the house showed its age. Still, to me, it was a mansion.

I walked down the street for a block, and already, my feet ached. I looked back at the Wesley House, and as soon as I was far away enough that I was sure the nuns could not see me, I kicked off my shoes and placed them under my arm. I stretched and wiggled my red toes and was relieved to feel the damp side-walk under them.

The first place the nuns had told me to visit was an open field with old, rusty train cars scattered about. Stacks of flat rocks and bricks supported the corners of each weather-beaten boxcar, allowing for living space under-neath. People had hung canvas over the lower living area for privacy and had placed tin buckets filled with plants and flowers around the outside.

I greeted a young woman sitting on the wooden steps in front of one of the boxcars. She nursed a baby while a group of small boys, some naked, ran around the box-cars chasing after a goat.

"Buenos días," she said, smiling.

"I'm looking for a place to live," I said and moved out of the way of the running kids. "Is there an empty boxcar my family and I can move into?"

The woman put the infant over her shoulder and shook her head. "No. Everyone here has a brother or a cousin waiting for a boxcar. Some have been waiting for months."

The group of small kids shouted and ran toward a line of tall trees that began at the far end of the lot. A breeze coming from that direction carried the damp smell of a creek.

"Have you tried *el avispero*," asked the woman, "the wasp's nest?"

I swallowed hard and shook my head. A place called *the wasp's nest* couldn't be good. Maybe people living there were mean, maybe their words or glares stung anyone who passed by.

"They call it el avispero because of the many families that live there—it's like a busy wasp's nest," the girl said. She gave me directions and told me about the old brown sign at the entrance of the alley. It advertised rooms with bed and stove for fifty cents a week.

I thanked the girl, and I as I walked through the rest of the neighborhood, past tiny, sad-looking homes, I understood why they called this place Los Corrales. It was because most homes resembled cattle pens. Most had never seen paint and shared the same gray, weather-stained color of a dreary, winter sky. Our adobe home in Esperanzas was humble, but it at least had appeared much happier and warmer than these shacks.

The second place the nuns had told me about was a lot with tiny wooden houses. Each stood shoulder to shoulder with barely enough space for a man to walk between them.

"Buenos días," I said to an old woman tending some potted plants in the front yard.

The old woman's eyes met mine. Her gaze then swept down to my scarf, to the shoes under my arm, and finally to my bare feet. She turned back to her plants. "What do you want?"

"I'm..." I cleared my throat. "I'm looking for a place to—"

"The Wesley House sent you, right?" the woman asked.

"Yes, ma'am. And they—"

"Hush!" said the woman, without looking at me. "I have nothing available. Tell the Wesley House to stop sending people."

I stood quiet for a moment, thinking of what to say next.

"Didn't you hear me?" she said, turning to me this time. "I've got nothing!"

I wished the woman a good day and turned away. By

this time, I wanted to go back to the Wesley House and call it a day, but something inside told me I had to stop at el avispero, the wasp's nest.

I prayed for better luck there.

fifteen

MISTER

I **stood in front of** el avispero, and nothing flew or buzzed through the air. The only sound came from the brown, rusted tin sign that creaked in the wind. I stared at the peeling white letters and symbols written on it. The only thing I could recognize was the number fifty.

I walked under the sign and into the alley. To my left was a row of tiny shacks, side by side, all strung together like the boxcars of a train. The shacks appeared smaller than any of the houses I'd seen earlier, but their run-down color—the sad gray—was the same.

Each shack, despite its small size, had its own tiny porch, and on each porch were people working. One man assembled birdcages using bamboo sticks. He chatted with his neighbor, who wiggled his fingers fast over a table as he rolled each cigarette made of corn husks.

Women ground corn and cooked tortillas, and others scrubbed clothes against a washboard in large tin baths. Along the walls and over the doors of most shacks hung batches of dried meat, strings of peppers, and wet clothes.

The day had warmed, and the sense that my clothes were sticking to my body felt strange. Unlike back home in Esperanzas, the air here was different. It felt wet.

"*Buenas tardes*," I said to one of the women. "I'm looking for a place to live. Who do I speak to?"

"To Mister Bob," said a young mother nursing her baby. "He lives in number fourteen." She pointed to a shack behind me that stood alone, halfway down the alley, with its door wide open.

The name sounded strange. I repeated it. "Mister Bob?"

The girl nodded.

I reached the shack branded with the number fourteen over its doorway. Beyond the open door sat a white man at a table, gnawing on an ear of corn. His hair and his thick beard were the color of fire. He looked like a big man, and I'd hate to get him upset.

I took a deep breath and stepped onto the porch. He glanced up and quickly put the corn down in his bowl. He stood, wiping his hands across his round belly.

"*Hola*," he said in Spanish.

"Mister Bob?" I asked.

"That's me. How can I help you?" His Spanish was much better than the nuns at the Wesley House.

I stood quietly and leaned my head back, taking in the size of the redheaded man. He was a bear.

"I'm looking for a place to live."

Mr. Bob stuck his head out the door and looked around.

"Where're your folks?"

I shook my head. "No folks. It's only me, my grandmother, and my two siblings."

"Are your folks still in Mexico? In the revolution?"

Without saying anything, I lowered my eyes and nodded.

Mr. Bob shook his head. "It's a shame," he said. "Such a beautiful place. I lived down there in a town called Monclova for years but had to leave when it all started." After a long sigh, Mr. Bob's smile returned. "Let me show you the rooms I have."

I let Mr. Bob lead the way. "Your sign says you have rooms for fifty cents, right?"

Mr. Bob, picking his tooth with his pinky, shook his head. "The last one was taken a week ago. But I have two more that cost a little more."

"How much?"

"One costs a dollar twenty-five a week and the other a dollar fifty."

I stopped walking. "That's more than twice what the sign says."

Mr. Bob chuckled. "Don't worry," he said. "We'll work something out."

We passed two tiny shacks with huge puddles in front of them. Long planks lay across the mud and puddled water, leading to each of their doors.

"This first one is the outhouse," said Mr. Bob. "It has a flushable toilet."

I could already hear Amelia's excitement about having a flushable toilet. That was, if we could afford this place.

"The other one has a shower bath." Mr. Bob looked

back at me. "There's a time limit for the shower. Otherwise, people stay in there forever."

Mr. Bob went over to the row of shacks and opened the door to one of them. The two rooms inside, like his shack, had no windows. I followed through the doorway and was surprised to see the shack was as deep as a train car. The ceiling was a different story. It barely cleared Mr. Bob's height.

There was a brass bed and a small old dresser in the first room. The curtain that separated the rooms was halfway pulled back, and I could see a stove toward the back of the second room.

My heart raced with the possibility of living here, but I reminded myself of the price.

"I have a strict rule," Mr. Bob said. "I don't allow animals. No goats, no dogs, no birds—nothing."

"We have none, sir," I said.

"I also ask my tenants to clean their rooms thoroughly once a week. Everything has to be put out in the sun, and the floors have to be scrubbed."

I had noticed that everything around me looked rundown but clean and orderly.

"Do you like it?" asked Mr. Bob.

I nodded with a sigh, wishing I had a way to pay for it.

"How much money do you have?"

"None, sir," I said. "We just got here yesterday."

Mr. Bob, pulling at his beard, stared at me as if expecting an answer to a question.

I looked down at my hands and my fingers then rubbed them together, thinking what to say.

Finally, I spoke up. "I'm a quick learner, and a hard worker too. I know I'll find work soon."

Mr. Bob smiled. "Now you're talking. What kind of work have you done before?"

"I used to chop wood and sell it in my village. I could buy an ax and—"

Mr. Bob shook his head. "I'm not sure you've noticed, but the only trees around here are the ones down by the creek. Anyhow, people here don't use wood."

I looked out to the sun beaming on the alley's muddy ground, trying to think of something else.

"Here's the deal. You can stay here one week, and I'll help you find work. But by next week, I'll need this week's rent plus the next in advance from your first pay. *De acuerdo?* Is that a deal?"

I nodded repeatedly before he could change his mind.

"*Muchas gracias*, Señor Mister Bob," I said. "Thank you very much."

Confused, Mr. Bob looked at me then chuckled. "The word *mister* means *señor* in English."

Now I was the one puzzled. "So *Mister* is not your first name?"

"No, it's Bob, but congratulations!" Mr. Bob clapped "You've learned your first word in English."

My cheeks grew hot as I looked down at my bare feet.

I rushed out of the wasp's nest without being stung and as happy as could be.

sixteen
FIRST GUESTS

Abuelita crossed herself as she walked through the door of our new home. "M'ija, can we afford this?"

"We will next week," I said, stretching to grab the string hanging from the light bulb. I pulled on the string, and when the light came on, it gave the room a warm glow.

"Is this a bed?" asked Amelia. She ran her hands across the white iron loops at the foot of it. "It's beautiful!"

We all took turns sitting on it and laughed at the way it squeaked every time we moved. In no time, Amelia kicked off her shoes and began jumping on it like a grasshopper on fire. Luisito, with eyes wide open, bounced around as he clung to the bed's brass post.

"Stop, Amelia. You're going to break it," I said, walking toward the curtain that divided the room.

When I pulled the flowery curtain back, I saw the same rusty stove I'd seen the day before. This time, though, I noticed new things—a small table, three chairs, and a small loft.

Sitting on the floor, next to the stove, was a metate and two large bamboo crates filled with earthenware.

I reached for the light bulb string hanging above the table and noticed the short and narrow stairs that led to the loft.

The dark planks above us creaked, making us look up. Amelia ran to Abuelita.

"Is someone up there?" Abuelita asked.

"I don't know," I said, taking the first step up the screeching stairs.

"Be careful, Petra," said Amelia. "Remember the creek we passed? Maybe it's *la llorona*. Maybe she lives up there." If there was something Amelia feared more than the dark, it was the weeping woman who wandered down creeks and rivers, crying for her missing children.

"If la llorona lives up there, she owes me half the rent," I said, taking the next step.

Suddenly, a head peeked out from the loft.

Amelia yelped. I jumped back, lost my balance, and fell to the floor.

"Buenas," said a young woman. "You must be the new tenants."

The woman had a beaming smile, but it soon vanished when she realized I was on the floor. "Oh, my goodness. Did I startle you?" She ran down the stairs to help me up. "Are you alright? I'm so sorry."

"I'm fine," I said, taking her hand.

"Who are you?" asked Abuelita.

"I'm Camila, your neighbor," said the woman. "*Para servirle.*"

A little girl, younger than Amelia, took careful steps as she came down from the loft. Amelia slowly let go of Abuelita's waist as she observed the little girl.

"And this is Nina," said Camila, "my daughter." Nina sheepishly hid behind her mother's skirt. "We live upstairs, in the attic," said Camila.

I hadn't known there was an attic. That explained why the ceiling was so low.

"Pleased to meet you, Doña Camila," said Abuelita.

"Please, just call me Camila. The word *doña* makes me feel old. I'm only twenty."

We all introduced ourselves to Camila and her daughter, Nina, and invited them to sit on our chairs as our very first guests.

"How much do you pay in rent?" I asked.

"Fifty cents a week," said Camila. "For fifty cents I get to sleep upstairs and use the stove. Though I don't use it much since I always bring cooked food from my job. I work for a *reina*, a chili queen downtown."

"A chili queen? What's that?" asked Abuelita.

"They're women who run open-air restaurants in the plazas," Camila said. "They set up right before dusk and run their stands into the night. They serve all kinds of Mexican food, but their main dish is chili meat. I'm a waitress and take customer's orders."

"Who watches Nina when you work?" asked Abuelita.

"There's an old woman who sits at the metate all evening grinding corn, and Nina usually sits by her. When it's late, Nina rolls out a *tapete* and sleeps until I'm done working."

"From now on, leave Nina with us," said Abuelita. "She and Amelia could play and help me watch after Luisito."

Camila's face lit up. "Thank you, señora. Thank

you very much. It'll help tremendously." She turned to her daughter. "Did you hear that, Nina? You can stay with them while Mama works." Nina pressed her lips together and turned to Amelia.

"Can I show Nina our bed?" asked Amelia.

Abuelita nodded.

"No jumping on it," I said.

Amelia rolled her eyes and took Nina by the hand, "Come with me, Nina. Let me show you the bed we can never, ever jump on."

Smiling, Camila turned to me. "Petra, have you found work?"

"No, ma'am," I said.

"The chili queen I work for may have something," Camila said. "How about you come with me this afternoon? If she likes you, she may hire you on the spot."

seventeen
HER MAJESTY

Late that afternoon I showered and combed my hair into a tight ponytail. I wore the nice clothes the Wesley House had given me—a brown wool skirt that reached halfway down my shins and a white-buttoned blouse with an open collar. I tied my purple scarf around my neck and put the dreadful shoes on. This time, though, I placed small scraps of fabric around my toes to keep my blisters from rubbing against the shoes.

Camila and I walked away from the wasp's nest and turned the corner toward the main street.

"That's our trolley!" said Camila. "*Córrele!* Run!"

As a little girl, I had always enjoyed running as fast as I could, barefoot, across the hot desert ground. Now, with feet crammed inside these shoes, I felt clumsy and could barely keep up with Camila.

The trolley's brass bell rang, and its brakes screeched as it reached the stop before us. Camila waved her arms at the trolley as it waited patiently for us to board.

Laughing and catching her breath, Camila dropped two coins into a glass box. "One for you and one for me," she said.

"I owe you," I told her, catching my breath too.

She shook her head and waved at me. "Don't worry about it."

I followed Camila down the aisle, and we both sat on the farthest bench in the back.

"You know what I've learned since living here?" said Camila. "I've learned that you spend a lot of time looking for work, and once you find it, you spend a lot of time worrying how to keep it."

The fear of losing a job I didn't have yet was silly, but still, the thought made my stomach turn. Instinctively, I reached for my black rock, but it wasn't there. My heart sank when I didn't feel it. Quickly, I reached into my other pocket until I remembered I had left it in my old skirt.

"Are you all right?" asked Camila. "Did you lose something?"

I sighed and shook my head. "I'm all right."

The trolley drove out of our neighborhood, Los Corrales, and into a part of the city I'd never seen. There were red, yellow, brown, and ivory buildings, some as tall as four, five, and even ten windows high.

The trolley's brass bell rang, and Camila stood, saying it was our stop.

"There are many chili queens in town," said Camila, "But the one I work for, Doña Carmen, reigns over Alamo Plaza. It's a ten-minute walk from here."

We walked past a cathedral and a tall, red stone building. The sidewalks here were wider than back at Los Corrales, and they were filled with people speaking strange tongues—some rang harsh while some sounded choppy, a lot different than the soft shush sounds of English.

People of all shapes, sizes, and colors passed us. The white women who wore fancy silk dresses pushed their babies in white carts lined with lace. Then there were women who wore colorful satin robes and wooden sandals. They wore their dark hair in large puffs held up with wooden sticks that looked like pencils. These women—who Camila said were *chinas*, Chinese—didn't push babies on carts; they carried them on their backs, like us. The sidewalks were also crowded with cowboys and Mexican people who were either dressed like me or in the same kind of fancy silks the rich women wore back home.

"Always address the chili queen as *Doña Carmen*," said Camila. "Always."

Camila stopped and faced me as people walked around us. "And something else. This is important. If Doña Carmen speaks to you, don't ask about food, wages, paydays, or anything of that sort. Otherwise you spoil your chances of getting hired. Understood?"

I nodded.

During our hurried walk, I caught glimpses of store-front windows that displayed waxlike figures of women wearing elegant silks and plumes. And just as elegant were the American flags that waved freely on many rooftops and store entrances, reminding me of the day I had crossed the bridge from Mexico.

Camila and I crossed a tall metal bridge, and as soon as we turned the corner, she pointed to a patch of green-ery ahead of us.

"That's Alamo Plaza," she said.

Alamo Plaza was a small island surrounded by tall, colorful buildings and cobblestone streets. Automobiles, buggies, and wagons lined the edge of the plaza, and in its center stood a bandstand, not much bigger than the one we had in my hometown.

"Does the chili queen sit inside the bandstand?" I asked. I imagined her sitting on a throne, overlooking the entire plaza.

"No. She sets up just north of the plaza."

We walked all along the edge of the plaza, until we reached a group of people who were unloading tables and pots of food from wagons.

Camila grabbed my hand and guided me toward a plump lady who stood with her hands on her hips, talking to a man in one of the wagons.

"Food first. You know better," said the plump lady to the man "Did you not hear me the first time? Were you not listening?"

Camila cleared her throat. "Doña Carmen," she said and let go of my hand. "Good afternoon, ma'am." Camila nudged me with her elbow to step closer.

"This here is Petra and...she needs a job," Camila

said, fumbling with the end of her shawl. "I told her you might be hiring."

Doña Carmen stood shorter than Camila and me, but she had strong, broad shoulders. She wore a white embroidered dress, cinched at the waist by a bright red apron. There was a large corsage of roses pinned to her chest, and her hair, braided thick with vibrant ribbons, sat like a crown atop her head.

Doña Carmen sighed heavily and looked over at me. "Have you worked at a chili stand before?" she asked.

"No, ma'am, but I've done other things," I said.

"Like what?" asked Doña Carmen.

"Back home I chopped firewood and sold it in my village," I said.

Doña Carmen's face changed. She appeared interested. "Can you lift heavy things?"

I responded without thinking twice. "Yes, ma'am."

"Let me see your hands," said the chili queen.

I lifted my palms for her to see.

Doña Carmen nodded in approval. "You have nice, strong calloused hands." She then looked me in the eye.

"Can you read?" asked the chili queen.

My answer didn't come as quick this time. "No," I

said, looking down at my feet, then quickly pulled my chin up. "Not yet, ma'am. But I will, soon."

"My family has been running this chili stand for three generations," said Doña Carmen. "I can't afford to hire people who won't work hard for me."

Reaching into her embroidered apron, Doña Carmen pulled out a cigarette. She lit it and took a long drag. She then released the smoke to the sky and looked at me.

"I'm a loyal queen," said Doña Carmen. "If you work hard for me and prove your loyalty, I'll take care of you." She took the cigarette back to her lips and took a second puff. "Are you willing to work hard?"

"Yes, ma'am," I said. "I can cook, clean—whatever you need me to do."

Doña Carmen nodded, flicking the ashes onto the ground. "You could help me set up the tables and clean during and after we're done. You can also help Camila serve food. In time I'll send you to run errands."

I didn't know what to say. All I could do was nod and smile.

"I'll pay you sixty cents for a full day's work. Can you start now?"

My heart almost jumped out of my chest with her

words. I kept my hands on my sides but squeezed them tight into fists, ready to work.

"Yes," I said. "I mean, yes, ma'am." I looked over at Camila, who had a beaming smile that reflected mine.

Darkness gathered above us as tiny light bulbs that hung around the plaza lit the night like summer fireflies. Each table, decorated with a pyramid of glassware, also had tall red, yellow, and green lanterns.

When I wasn't cleaning the tables or gathering the dirty plates, I helped Camila serve food. Some food I'd seen before, like beans, tortillas, stuffed peppers, enchiladas, Mexican rice, and *sopa de oro*. Chili, the main dish, was a food I'd never seen before. It was a thick, reddish beef stew. For dessert we served *pan dulce*, Mexican pastries, and *champurrado*, a cornmeal gruel drink mixed with chocolate. We also served tea, coffee, beer, mescal, pulque, and lots and lots of water.

The customers were courteous and included rich and poor, young and old, brown and white. There were plenty of Anglos who seemed to really enjoy the food. Some, though, appeared to be new to it. Using their silverware, they'd examine the chili and tortillas before tasting them, and as they chewed, they'd nod in approval at the person next to them, when suddenly, a shade of red would transform their faces into pain. These customers always screamed for water and easily chugged down three pitchers for every bowl of chili they ate. I quickly came to learn that the word for *agua* in English was *water.*

The smell of roasted garlic and chili filled the night breeze, and as I wiped the tables clean, I looked around at every glowing sign. The biggest one was a sign of a cowboy lassoing a steer. Its blue, white, and golden glow glistened over the bright jewels the women sitting at the tables wore. Sounds came from every direction—iron shoes clomping against the cobblestones, automobiles honking and bells from streetcars ringing. There was music from the bandstand and laughter from all the people eating at the stand. It was truly spellbinding—like one big celebration.

"What did you think of your first night?" asked Camila, stretching her neck from side to side.

"My feet are killing me," I said, shaking out the tablecloths as I folded them. "But I enjoyed it."

After I helped load the last table onto the wagon, Doña Carmen approached me.

"Good work, *muchacha*," she said, pulling a folded handkerchief out of her bosom. "Here's your money." Doña Carmen counted by fives as she placed twelve coins in my hand. "We'll see you here tomorrow at the same time."

I nodded repeatedly and wrapped my fingers around the coins.

Camila and I turned the corner away from Alamo Plaza to head home. As we passed under a wide arch, hung with bright bulbs that illuminated the street, I stopped to remove my shoes. All the blisters had popped open. The pain seemed worse after removing my shoes despite the relief of having them off. Still, I couldn't keep from smiling.

"If I work..." I said, looking out into the dark quiet street. "Wait...how many nights a week will I be working?"

"Typically, we work six nights," Camilla said.

I quickly added up the money I could possibly earn in one week. Between foot cramps and bleeding blisters, I limped, holding on to Camila's shoulder. My heart raced as I thought about the money I'd make in one month or one year.

By the time Camila and I got off the streetcar, my feet were feeling better. Still, she insisted on carrying both bowls of chili the queen had given us.

"I didn't realize people could drink that much water in one sitting," I said.

Camila threw her head back, laughing. "It never fails. I always tell the queen she should charge tourists for water instead of food."

Camila and I entered our alley and noticed Mister Bob sitting in a chair on his porch, his feet propped up on a crate.

He tipped his cowboy hat as we walked by. "*Buenas noches*," he said.

"Buenas noches," Camila and I replied.

"Did you find a job?" Mister Bob asked.

"Yes, sir," I said. "I started tonight."

Mister Bob smiled, lifting his drink to me.

I was on top of the world that night. I was living my dream. All I needed for the dream to be complete was for Papa to be back in our lives.

eighteen

THE SLATE

Three weeks had passed since the queen had hired me. I worked for her six nights a week. Some mornings I worked for her sister, who ran a smaller stand at la Plaza del Zacate, the Haymarket Plaza. At the Haymarket, we served pan dulce, tacos, and coffee to men stopping by before work or to cowboys who were passing through.

My earnings added up to a little over five dollars a week while Amelia and Abuelita together earned about a dollar a week from shelling pecans at home and selling them to bakeries and candy factories. With our money we paid Mister Bob and bought groceries from Don Wong, a Chinese man who ran a shop a block away from our house.

Don Wong's store was about three times the size of

our shack. Rows of crates in the middle of the store displayed squash, peppers, onions, apples, and oranges, while clusters of bananas hung above them. From the ceiling too hung brooms, tin buckets, pots and pans, and upside-down umbrellas. Cans and boxes of all shapes and sizes filled almost every shelf on the walls. Their bright, colorful labels told us their contents—soup, beans, sardines, milk, soap, prunes, oats, and cereals.

"*Es todo?*" Don Wong would ask in Spanish every time we took our groceries to the counter. He spoke Spanish well, but when he spoke, he only said two or three words at a time.

As usual, I'd nod, and Don Wong, from behind the counter, would pull out a small book, a pencil, and an abacus. Wide-eyed, Amelia and I always stared at Don Wong as his fingers fiddled over the abacus, striking each bead swiftly, like hungry chickens pecking at grains. He'd then wet the pencil tip with his tongue and write down the totals in his book.

Amelia's eyes barely reached the top of the counter, but once Don Wong was done writing our totals, Amelia would stand on her toes, anticipating her pilón from Don Wong. The pilón, the small gift, was a piece of barrel candy Don Wong pressed into her hand to thank us for shopping at his store.

One day, while Amelia waited for her pilón, I looked at the strange red dragons that decorated the shelf behind him. I also looked at the strings of red beads that hung above the doorway separating the store from where Don Wong and his family lived. From time to time, I'd hear the language spoken by Don Wong's family. The sounds coming from behind the curtain always fascinated me and made me wish I could learn it.

"Look, Petra!" Amelia pointed to a shelf behind the counter.

Displayed on the shelf was the most beautiful writing slate. I'd been taught to write my name on one like it, except this one had a small, colorful abacus like Don Wong's, and its frame was decorated with neatly marked letters and numbers. On the bottom corner was a string attached to a slate pencil.

"Can we buy it one day?" said Amelia. "You can use it to learn to write, and me too. Oh, and so can Nina."

I looked back at the slate. It looked so shiny, so smooth, and so perfect.

"Cuánto?" I asked Don Wong, pointing to the slate. "How much?"

Don Wong, holding Amelia's pilón, turned back.

"Twenty-five cents," said Don Wong.

I pulled my head back. "Twenty-five?"

"Is that a lot?" asked Amelia.

I nodded. "That's about three hours' worth of work, and we just bought Abuelita's medicines too. Maybe next week."

"But what if it's gone?" said Amelia.

"No worry," said Don Wong, shaking his head. He then moved the slate to show us there were three more lying behind it.

Amelia smiled and sighed.

When we reached our small porch, Amelia ran in and shouted, "Abuelita, Abuelita, Petra and I just saw—"

"Petra," Abuelita interrupted, "did you give Don Wong the soap wrapper?"

I made a hissing sound through my teeth. "I'm sorry, I forgot."

"Well, make sure you don't lose it," Abuelita said. Soap wrappers had become a fascination for her since she learned she could exchange them for small prizes.

"Petra forgot about the soap wrapper because we saw the prettiest thing in the world," said Amelia. "It was a slate, Abuelita, and it had letters, numbers, and one of those things Don Wong uses to add up our groceries. It costs twenty-five cents."

"Twenty-five?" Abuelita said, crossing herself. "That's ten soaps."

Amelia turned to me. "Maybe we can help you buy it with the money Abuelita and I make from the pecans."

"No," I said. "We need to save money. The chili queen is teaching me how to be smart with it and how not to spend it on foolish things."

"The slate is not foolish," said Amelia. "It's going to teach you how to write."

"It's foolish when you barely have enough money for food and rent," I said, and immediately realized how I had sounded. I did want to learn to read and write, but the chili queen was teaching me how to work hard and save money in case hard times lay ahead.

"And my medicines too," Abuelita said. "Those are

expensive. Besides, Petra doesn't need to learn how to read anymore. She already has a great job."

I was about to roll my eyes, just like the chili queen often did with her workers. Instead, I shut them for a moment and took a deep breath. "Doña Carmen is very successful. She's been running the food stand for many years and brings in a lot of money because she's smart and because she knows how to read and add and multiply numbers. That's why she's successful."

"There's a lot about the chili queen you don't know yet," said Camila. Her voice was calm, but her eyes shot me a warning glance.

"I know enough," I said. "She has my loyalty, and in return she said she's going to teach me everything there is to know about making money."

Camila shrugged and walked away. Abuelita remained silent and sat at the table where she and Amelia began to shell pecans.

I sorted and stored the groceries. Afterward, I began getting ready for work. It was my day off, but I knew that showing up for work was one way to prove my loyalty to the chili queen, and with time, I knew I'd win hers.

nineteen

BLUE-STRIPED OVERALLS

The first lesson the chili queen had taught me was that everyone in life had a designated place, just like the patrons at her stand.

The long tables at the chili stand were set up as three large squares. Inside each large square was a smaller square of tables where certain patrons sat. These patrons included newspaper reporters, cowboys, gamblers, musicians, entertainers and actresses that worked at the opera house down the street. According to Doña Carmen, these customers always brightened the mood of the stand and also left nice gratuities. They were not as attached to their money as the patrons who sat on the outer tables, the city officials, sheriffs, judges, and laborers.

"Make sure you serve the freshest food and coffee to the inner square patrons," she often advised. "And don't forget to smile big for them too."

This night was slow because it was the first cool night of the season.

"It looks like it's only sheriffs and laborers tonight," said Doña Carmen, lighting up a cigarette.

"Will it be this slow from now on?" I asked.

Doña Carmen shook her head, releasing a puff of smoke into the air. "People will get used to the cool weather. It'll pick up again." She looked at me before putting the cigarette back to her lips. "How are we on coffee and corn?"

"We have plenty, ma'am," I said. "I checked everything, and we should be good for tonight."

Nodding, Doña Carmen threw the cigarette to the ground and stepped on it. "You're a good worker," she said. "You're smart too. It didn't take you long to figure out how to take orders, serve food, and run errands."

The wind had made me feel cold through the evening, but the queen's praises quickly warmed me up.

She then added another compliment that almost put me on fire. "Pretty soon you'll be able to help me run this place."

I took a deep breath and pressed my lips together to keep from jumping with excitement.

"Here." Doña Carmen pulled out the folded handkerchief from her chest and handed it to me. "Go count it and log it in the book."

"Want me to give it to your husband, or do I bring it back to you?" Don Lalo, the chili queen's husband, was a quiet man with a droopy mustache who worked near the wagons chopping food and washing dishes.

"Give it to my husband," she said. "You can go home afterward."

"Yes, ma'am," I said.

"One more thing," Doña Carmen said. "Tell Camila she can have Saturday off."

"Saturday?" I asked. "*Día de los Muertos*? The Day of the Dead?"

Doña Carmen nodded, "Both of you can have the day off."

I nodded, turning away, and didn't tell her that I'd probably still show up for work. I unfolded the handkerchief as I walked toward the wagons when I heard someone shout out my name.

I stopped. It was a familiar voice. No, I told myself.

It couldn't be who I thought it was. For a moment, I believed the howling wind was playing tricks on me.

Then I heard it again.

"Petra!"

I turned, and across the chili stand stood a young man, waving his arms at me. He wore blue-striped over-alls, a blue shirt, and a red scarf knotted around his neck.

It was my cousin Pablo.

My hands flew to my mouth in disbelief. The last time I'd heard anything about him was when Abuelita told me he had joined the rebels, right before the Federales burned down our village.

My eyes widened and blinked several times; I thought it was just my imagination. I had to get closer to prove my eyes wrong. I had to hold him to prove my heart right.

twenty

VANISHED

My chest swelled with joy, and my legs took off running on their own toward Pablo. Pablo rushed my way, but before I could reach him, my ankle popped to the side, and I fell to the ground on one knee. I felt embarrassed and in pain, but not enough to keep me on the ground.

"You clumsy girl," Pablo said upon reaching me.

I threw my arms around him without saying a word. Pablo squeezed me just as tight, almost lifting me off the ground.

We let go of each other, both of us laughing through tears. I had so much to say, so many questions to ask, but the knot in my throat wouldn't let me.

"Will you stop crying?" said Pablo, sniffing and smiling. He used his sleeve to wipe away tears.

"You started it," I said.

"Look at you," said Pablo, stepping back. "You're wearing shoes!" He threw his head back, laughing.

"That's why I fell," I said. "I can't run in these silly things."

Pablo narrowed his eyes on my neck. "And that purple scarf—I cannot wait to hear the story behind that."

I laughed and brushed away tears, happy to see that Pablo was as warm and lighthearted as always. The revolution had not changed him.

I finally managed to ask, "What happened to you?"

"What *didn't* happen to me," said Pablo.

"Have you seen my papa?" I asked.

Pablo's smile faded. He sighed and shook his head. "I've been looking for him. I've asked around but haven't found him. At least not yet. But don't worry." Pablo patted my shoulder. "Many people are finding each other—just like I found you. How are Abuelita, Amelia, and Luisito? Did you make it out all right?"

"We're all fine," I said. "How did you find me?"

"I work for the train company, and everywhere I go, I ask for you and *mi tío*. Today I had breakfast at the Haymarket and was told that a Petra Luna worked there sometimes. They also told me you worked at Alamo Plaza. I didn't want to get my hopes up, though."

"Why not?"

"Do you realize how many Petra Lunas are out there?" Pablo made a whistling sound. "None as clumsy as you, though!"

"Ay, *cállate*." I gave Pablo a gentle shove. "Hush."

"Are you working right now?" Pablo asked. "Can you take a break?"

I stopped and looked around, trying to remember what I was doing. "Actually, the chili queen said I was free to go. All I have to do is—"

The blood drained from my face as I remembered the handkerchief Doña Carmen had given me.

I quickly searched my pockets, but they were empty.

I looked behind me, forcing my eyes to quickly adjust to the darkness on the ground as they retraced my path, but nothing. No white, embroidered handkerchief, no coins, no bills—nothing. I felt my arms, my shoulders, my whole body turn limp.

"What's the matter?" asked Pablo.

My shaky hand went to the side of my face, and I managed to say, "I've let down the queen."

twenty-one

BUÑUELOS AND HANDKERCHIEFS

"Breathe," Pablo said and placed his hand on my shoulder. "It'll be all right. We'll find it."

Pablo and I retraced my path. We got on our hands and knees to search the area where I had tripped. We also went near the wagons to the spot where I'd first heard Pablo call my name.

Pablo sat on his haunches and turned to me. "Maybe we should ask the chili queen if someone—"

"No," I said right away. "Doña Carmen can't find out, otherwise she won't trust me anymore." Frustration knotted my insides. I wanted to scream and pull my hair out.

"How about we ask someone else?"

I too sat on my haunches and took in a deep breath. Part of me was tempted to take a peek at the chili queen and try to figure out if she knew, but I feared that if our eyes met, mine would give away what had happened.

I looked over at the people working in the kitchen near the wagon: the chili queen's husband, his two helpers, the girl serving, and the queen's mother, Doña Fina, whose tiny and feeble body sat at the metate.

"Doña Fina," I said, sheepishly. "I...uh..." My clasped hands pressed and rubbed against each other.

Doña Fina narrowed her small, tired eyes at me and suddenly smiled, "Petra, m'ija, it's you."

"Yes, it is," I said, smiling back at her. "Have you seen a folded handkerchief?"

"A what?" she said, bringing her hand to her ear.

I grew nervous. I didn't want others to hear. I turned to Pablo. He motioned me with his chin to try again.

I stooped. "Un pañuelo, Doña Fina. Have you seen a handkerchief on the ground or anywhere else?"

"Un buñuelo?" she said, almost shouting.

Pablo's clenched hand flew to his mouth as if trying to keep a burp from coming out, but I knew better. Unlike Pablo, I didn't find it funny that Doña Fina had misheard pañuelo for buñuelo, fried dough.

"No, Doña Fina," I said kneeling by her. "Un pañuelo," I said, drawing a square in the air with both of my index fingers.

"Ah, un pañuelo," she said and gave a bashful smile. "*A ver*," she said, putting the stone down on the metate and looking at the ground around her. She then tilted her head up to the sky with eyes shut, thinking hard, as if she'd been asked what she'd had for breakfast a month ago.

"Someone found something..." she said, "and I believe they gave it to Lalo."

I turned to Don Lalo, the chili queen's husband. He stood about twenty steps away with his back toward us. His right arm made strong, swift motions as he chopped the raw chili meat.

"Gracias, Doña Fina," I said.

"*Que Dios te bendiga*, m'ija," Doña Fina said, and I hoped her blessing would help me find the money.

Pablo waited for me while I approached Don Lalo, who grabbed handfuls of raw cubed meat and tossed them into a huge iron pot.

The chili queen's laugh, carried by the cool breeze, made me turn in her direction. She patted the back of a young cowboy who often frequented the stand.

Don Lalo's eyes had also turned to her but just as quickly shifted back to the meat he chopped.

Not once had I heard Don Lalo speak. It seemed as if the queen spoke for him.

"Don Lalo," I said. "Have you..."

His dark, intense eyes glanced at me. I could never tell if he was upset or just tired. I cleared my throat. "I lost a folded handkerchief. Have you seen it?"

Don Lalo's gaze dropped to the left side of his wooden cutting block, on a scrunched-up rag. When I hesitantly reached for it, he nodded.

The rag was speckled with tiny pieces of meat that had jumped from the wooden block every time Don Lalo's heavy knife thumped against it, but under it lay a pristine embroidered handkerchief. It was folded too. I grabbed it and turned back to Don Lalo to thank him, but his eyes had turned back to his task. I opened the handkerchief, and warmth swept through me when I saw money inside it.

"Gracias, Don Lalo," I said. "Where did you find it?"

Without looking at me, Don Lalo shrugged. I wanted to ask more questions. I wanted to ask who'd found it. I wanted to know if all the money had been returned or if some had been lost. But my questions would probably go unanswered.

"You found it," said Pablo. "Is all the money still there?"

"I hope so," I said.

I counted the money, logged in the queen's totals, and gave it all back to Don Lalo. As usual, he nodded once I told him the money was secure inside the tin box under his counter.

"Do you want to go see Abuelita?" I asked Pablo. "She would be so happy to see you."

Pablo pulled a silver watch from his pocket.

I gasped. "That's a really nice watch."

Pablo nodded. "Americans are as ingenious as they're wasteful. I found this at a dump, and it only cost me ten cents to fix it." He put the watch back in his pocket. "I have about an hour before my train departs. Do you live near?"

"No," I said sighing. "It takes me about thirty minutes to get home. You won't make it back in time."

"*Chihuahua*," Pablo grumbled. "I was hoping to see everyone, but if I'm late—even five minutes—they'll let me go. I'll come again next week, but tonight, I have an idea." He stepped closer with a mischievous smile and looked around as if about to share a secret. "Have you ever had an ice cream soda?"

twenty-two
DRUMMER BOY

The place Pablo took me to was dark and looked closed. Still, he looked through the glass window and knocked. A small light toward the back was turned off.

"What's this place?" I asked.

"My friend works here," said Pablo. "It's a confectionery store, a candy shop."

"But I don't like candies," I said.

Pablo cocked his head to one side. "Hmmm. I seem to remember someone who *always* begged me to share my *cajeta* with them, even after having eaten half of Amelia's. Wait a minute, that was you!"

I pushed Pablo with my elbow and chuckled. Warmth spread over me remembering those days. *Cajeta*, caramelized milk, was a treat Abuelita made for us every Christmas Eve.

"*Cajeta* is different," I said. "These American sweets are just too sweet for me, but you should see Amelia. Our neighbor Camila makes these round, flat cakes for breakfast, and Amelia always pours half a bottle of—"

"Karo syrup?" asked Pablo.

I nodded, surprised.

"That stuff is amazing!" said Pablo right as his friend opened the door and hushed us.

"Keep it down," Pablo's friend whispered. He was about Pablo's age, stocky, with a buttoned white shirt that almost matched his pale skin under the moonlight. He looked both ways down the street then waved us in.

I followed Pablo through the darkness, breathing in the air infused with vanilla. He led me up a grand staircase, and even in the darkness, I could see the polished wood around us.

As we stepped onto the second level of the store, Pablo's friend turned on the lights.

The room, much larger than the one we'd first came through, was as fancy as the first-class train we'd ridden on.

"Sit here," Pablo said, patting the stool next to him.

He introduced me to his friend, who called the place

where we were sitting a soda fountain counter. The friend opened and shut bottom cabinets and pulled on silver levers. He was scooping out something creamy from a tin container.

"Is it ready?" Pablo asked with a grin.

Pablo's friend nodded as he turned and set a tall crystal glass in front of me. He gently placed a long silver spoon next to it.

Inside the glass was a mountain of snow-like cream that oozed a brown, fizzy fluid from its peak. The goo turned into a beige foam as it sat at the brim of the glass.

"Go ahead," said Pablo. "Try it."

I grabbed the spoon and glanced at Pablo and his friend. Both looked at me with anticipation.

I lightly scraped the top part of the foam, but before I could taste it, Pablo took the spoon from me and shook his head.

"No," he said. "If you want to experience all that America has to offer, you're going to have to dig deep." Pablo shoved the spoon into the glass and scooped a huge spoonful of the white-and-brown mix. "Now try it," he said, handing me the dripping spoon.

I took a deep breath and put the spoon inside my mouth.

My eyes shut tight. It felt as if a torrent of sugar had been poured into my mouth while the sensation of tiny bees stinging my tongue and throat took over me.

Pablo and his friend broke into laughter as I kept one hand tight over my mouth and scrambled to find something to spit into. I looked at the counter, at the floor, but both were too pristine to spit on, so I did the unthinkable—I forced myself to swallow the whole thing.

"That was awful," I said, wiping my mouth with my sleeve.

"I agree," said Pablo's friend. "I don't see how these Americans and even this *tonto* here likes this kind of stuff." After handing me a glass of water, Pablo's friend took the float away and disappeared behind a swinging door near the corner of the room.

"You should have seen your face," said Pablo.

I pressed my lips together, starting to get annoyed. "I see you haven't changed much."

"Oh, I've changed a lot," said Pablo. "Probably the same way you have, and everyone else who's made it out of that hell."

He pushed himself away from the counter then leaned back against his stool and crossed his arms.

"For one thing, I don't see myself ever going back to Mexico."

Something inside me shriveled at his words. "Why not? That's our home."

Pablo chuckled, looking down at his calloused palms. "Mexico may have been our home, but it never belonged to us."

Growing up I always thought Pablo talked a lot about nothing, that the stuff he said never made sense. This time was different.

"Mexico belongs to the fancy, rich people who tell us how to live," said Pablo. "And they want us indios and mestizos to be happy and accept a life of misery and ignorance. When I close my eyes, I can still hear the priest from our hacienda telling us, 'If you obey *el hacendado*, the hacienda owner, God will see your humility and save your soul.' Yet el hacendado never cared about any of us. He worked my mother to death and then had my father executed for speaking out against him."

My jaw clenched. I knew Pablo had been orphaned at six years old, but I never knew how it had happened.

We both sat silent for a moment.

"Do you remember the first time my papa sat us down and told us about the revolution?" I asked.

Pablo nodded. "I'll never forget that evening because, for the first time, I had hope." He smiled. "When I joined the rebels, I wanted to be the best soldier they'd ever seen. When the trumpets sounded to signal a new battle, I'd run to the front as fast as I could and yell, *'Viva la revolución! Tierra y libertad!'*"

"Did you fight in a lot of battles?" I asked him.

Pablo's smile vanished, and his gaze dropped to the floor. He reached into his back pocket, pulled out his blue-striped cap, and placed it on the counter.

"Enough to make me rethink this whole revolution."

"How so?"

Pablo locked his eyes on his cap, and after a long sigh, he began to talk.

"The first three or four battles I fought were small. We won those easily. Then the Federales started coming in droves. Train after train full of them. My battle cries grew quieter when I noticed how disoriented the newly arrived Federales were. Many didn't even have a weapon, and those who did didn't even know how to load it, much less fire it. They looked lost, unwilling to fight. Still, I followed orders and charged."

"Then," Pablo continued, "there was this one battle where the Federales fired a cannon at us. Fortunately, we had just gotten one too. I hid behind a large stone, and every time the cannons blasted, I felt as if the ground would open and swallow us whole. When we finally were given the order to charge, I ran from behind the stone, holding my weapon, ready to kill the enemy, but then I stopped."

I lowered my eyes, not wanting to listen anymore. My own father was the enemy Pablo spoke of, and I pictured him in those same battles. I forced myself to speak. "Why did you stop?"

Pablo filled his lungs with air.

"The enemy," said Pablo, "was a young boy, not much older than me. He stood atop a boulder, waving a white flag. But then I looked at the ground."

Pablo shut his eyes and used his hands, now trembling, to hide his face. "Petra, I saw things...things I wished I'd never seen."

My hand reached over to Pablo's shoulder, hoping to comfort him.

"The ground was blood-soaked, and scattered around me were many bodies, all from the so-called other side. I was used to seeing blood and carnage, but for the first time, to my horror, I realized that most of the bodies were of children, all wearing the federal uniform. Most didn't even have a weapon. Some, as young as Amelia, had died holding each other.

"The world around me spun. I couldn't breathe. I wanted to run away from it all, even from my own flesh. I was about to lose my mind when I heard a cry."

Pablo's hands swept his face, and his red eyes were full of tears.

"I ran through the smoke," Pablo said, "toward the cry, tripping over bodies until I saw him—a little boy sitting in the middle of all that mess. His tiny arms squeezed around a small drum. He cried and rocked himself over it."

I covered my mouth in disbelief.

"I tore off my shirt and covered him, and after knocking that obnoxious uniform hat off, I carried him to our camp."

"Was he all right? Did he live?"

"By God's grace he didn't have more than a few scratches."

"How did he end up there?"

"The little boy told me his story as best as he could. He said he didn't know where he was from. All he could remember were the Federales storming the orphanage where he lived. They forced all the boys who were eight and older to join them. He said the nuns cried and begged for the smaller children to be spared, but the Federales threatened to kill them and burn down the orphanage."

"Monsters," I whispered.

Pablo nodded, squeezing his hands together. "That's the enemy I wanted to fight," said Pablo. "I didn't join to fight people like your papa and those children."

"What happened to the little boy?"

"There was a woman at our camp, a *soldadera,* who had lost all of her four small children. A few days after we took the boy to her, she was a different woman. It was like she'd seen the sun again after a long, harsh winter."

"I'm sorry for all you went through," I said.

"When I joined the rebels, I saw a lot of good men fighting, all for a good cause. Before long I noticed some men whose hearts weren't in the right place. They sowed division among the rebels, and soon I was fighting my own friends. It was hard to tell the good guys from the bad guys. It was all a blur as to whom we were fighting and why."

Pablo shook his head. "And the violence. So many lives wasted for nothing. It was then I realized that the war was never going to end. I wanted out."

"I can't blame you for not wanting to go back," I said. I told Pablo all about the Federales burning our home, about my encounter with Marietta, and about our escape from Mexico.

"Do you like it here, or do you think you'll go back one day?" asked Pablo.

"I really like it here. If I go back, it'll only be to find Papa. Once I find him, I'll come back with him."

Pablo looked at his watch. It was time for him to leave. We said our farewells to his friend and walked out of the candy shop. Outside, Pablo put on his hat and looked up at the stars. He took in a mouthful of the cool, crisp air.

"Thank you for listening, *prima*," said Pablo. "I feel better."

I smiled and nodded. "Me too."

With hands in his pockets, Pablo walked me all the way to my streetcar stop.

"Don't forget," he said, "tell Abuelita I'll be here next week, and make sure you tell her why I couldn't see her today."

"I will," I said. "The important thing is that we found each other."

Pablo smiled and stretched out his arms. I hugged him, trying to capture his warmth, trying to inhale the familiar scent of my old home. It pained me to let him go. And as I watched him walk away, I wondered if somewhere out there, maybe Papa was living the same nightmare Pablo had seen.

twenty-three
JUMPING GRASSHOPPERS

It was almost midday Saturday when I arrived home from a morning shift at the Haymarket.

I shut my eyes, hoping to get some rest before my shift with the chili queen, but thoughts of Mama and Papa crept into my head. Today was the start of Día de los Muertos. It was a day we went to the cemetery and celebrated the dead by treating them to their favorite food, singing their favorite songs, or putting out a piece of clothing or trinket that reminded us of them in some way. It was a time to share stories of them.

I had hoped to celebrate Mama's life this year, to honor her death, but she lay buried so far away, and in this new place, I had nothing that belonged to her—no shawl, no hair ribbons, nothing. And Papa, was he still alive? Pablo's stories of what he saw in the battlefields had brought me nightmares and spun webs of worry inside my head. My best hope was to go to work and focus on the chili queen's orders and her clients. That would make the day fly by without me thinking of life or death.

In the late afternoon, I showered and began getting ready for work. As usual, I combed and pulled my hair back in a ponytail. I tied my purple scarf around my neck and grabbed my black rock from the dresser. I gave it a good squeeze before putting in my pocket.

"Petra," said Camila, sticking her head in from the other room. "Can you help me carry the baskets of food and flowers to the cemetery tonight?"

"I can't," I said, turning back to the faded mirror and straightening my hair. "I work today."

"You're off today," said Camila. "The queen gave us both the day off."

"I know, but the chili queen might need me."

"If she needed you, she would've told you last night."

I kept my eyes on the mirror. "My grandmother can help you."

"She's carrying Luisito."

"Then have Amelia and Nina help you."

"They're carrying the candles. And besides, you know better. The girls can't carry the heavy baskets all the way to the cemetery."

I dropped my shoulders and turned to her, giving a heavy sigh. "Then have somebody else help you—a neighbor, or Mr. Bob. I need to work today. I need the money, and helping you carry those baskets won't get me paid."

As my last words came out, I looked up at Camila. She stared at me in silence. After a moment, she turned and walked away. I tried to shake off the bitter feeling inside me by sitting on the bed and lacing up my boots. I told myself it was pointless to go to the cemetery when neither Camila nor I had a loved one buried there.

Abuelita came into the small room and stood in front of me. She kept her hands inside the pockets of her apron.

"M'ija, you can't treat people that way, especially Camila."

"Treat her how?" I asked. "What's wrong with me going to work on my day off?"

Abuelita stayed quiet. She continued to stare at me as if I already knew the answer to my questions.

I shrugged and finished tying up both laces. "Camila needs to find someone else to help her." I tried to stand, but Abuelita pressed down on my shoulder.

"Aren't you glad Camila didn't say the same thing to you when you were looking for work? When we were all new here and didn't know how we were going to pay for this place?"

I lowered my gaze.

Abuelita kept her hand on my shoulder and supported herself to slowly sit next to me. "You're misguided, Petra. You're busy proving your loyalty to the chili queen, but it's your family, the people who care for you, like Camila, you owe your loyalty to."

"You don't understand," I said. "It's not about loyalty. It's about making money, paying the bills, your medicine—"

"M'ija"—Abuelita placed her hand on my lap—"it doesn't matter how much or how hard you work. When you disrespect people, things fall apart in the end. It's good to work hard, but family and loved ones should always come first."

I kept my mouth shut rather than to tell her that I thought Doña Carmen had done more for me than Camila.

"Go and apologize to Camila," said Abuelita.

I pressed my lips together and gave a slight nod. "Do I still have to help her carry the baskets?"

"That's up to you, m'ija. You're a young woman, and by now you should know what's right. All I ask is that you listen."

"Mira," said Abuelita. She grabbed my hand and pressed it against my gut, just below my chest. "When you're unsure about something or in a hurry to get somewhere, stop for a moment and place your hand here. Close your eyes, and in your mind, see yourself doing the things that are in question. When one choice makes you feel like there are a hundred *chapulines* inside your gut, trying to escape, then you have your answer. Go with what gives you peace."

I forced half a smile and nodded. I didn't want to shut my eyes or stop and feel for any grasshoppers jumping inside me.

"Both your gut and your heart will tell you what's best," said Abuelita. "But you must remain still and listen, otherwise you won't hear a single *chapulín*."

Abuelita's hand reached for my eyes, and in a sweeping motion, she asked me to shut them. "*Cierra los ojos.* Try it."

I sucked in a small breath and sat quietly, but not for long. The only thing I felt were my toes wiggling inside my shoes. My feet were itching to make their way to the chili queen.

"All right," I said, jumping to my feet. "I think I heard something."

"Good," said Abuelita. "Go on and apologize."

Out on the porch, Camila knelt next to a crib. It was a tiny white crib, perhaps too small for a baby, and it was decorated with red flowers and green strips of paper that interlaced the wooden rails like vines. Camila added another paper flower to it.

"Do you think it looks nice?" Camila asked. Her smile was back.

I nodded. Camila turned to the crib with a proud, beaming smile that made my chest feel tight.

"Was that Nina's crib?" I asked, hoping she'd nod.

Camila chuckled. "No, it's a doll crib. I bought it over a year ago. I've been decorating it a little at a time. It's for my son."

I looked at Camila. She had never mentioned a son. My heart sank as feelings of guilt erupted all over me. Guilt about not knowing more about Camila, guilt about not having listened. I remained quiet, not knowing what to say.

Camila turned to me. "About two years ago I gave birth to a beautiful boy, but nine months later, the Lord took him away."

"I'm sorry," I said. Looking back, I must have talked to Camila about the chili queen a thousand times— about how intelligent and good she was to me about how well she paid me, and about how much I wanted to be like her one day. Instead, I should have listened to Camila talk about her life, her dreams, and her sorrows. I looked down at the crib and felt the very first grasshopper jump inside the tightness in my chest.

"Last year was the first Day of the Dead since my son had passed," said Camila, "but Doña Carmen couldn't give me the day off. It broke my heart. I wanted to be there for his spirit's passage, but all I could do was get a friend to put a few marigolds over his grave."

"But this year," Camila continued with a glowing smile. "I want to decorate it with lots of marigolds, lots of candles. and this little crib. I also want to take him a sliced orange, his favorite crackers, and a bottle of milk."

Camila adjusted her skirt before continuing to

decorate the crib. I stood in silence, watching her roll each strip of green tissue paper and twist it around the rails of the crib.

I stood still and listened to my heart and gut. Ever since we'd left Mexico, I'd been dreading today—our first Day of the Dead since Mama's passing. It killed me that no one would be at Mama's grave to assure her passage and that I had nothing of Mama to hold or smell or to place on our *ofrenda*, our shrine at home. I also hated that Camila couldn't be there to welcome her baby's spirit the year before, and I wondered why the chili queen had not given her the time off. Surely, Doña Carmen couldn't be that coldhearted. Perhaps it was a busy weekend. But the more I thought about working on my day off, the more grasshoppers rattled inside me.

Camila reached down to one of the baskets sitting by the crib.

"I had this trinket made last month," she said, handing me a little glass bottle, small enough to sit in the palm of my hand. Inside were a tiny cross made from tin, a picture of the Virgin Mary holding baby Jesus, and lots of tiny paper flowers that resembled marigolds. The bottle was secured with a tiny cork.

I handed the bottle back to Camila. "I'll help you carry the baskets."

Camila looked at me with a hopeful smile and then shook her head as her eyes turned back to the crib. "Thank you. I'll just carry everything inside the crib. There's really no need for the two large baskets."

"You'll rip the paper flowers and the vines," I said. "Let me help you."

Camila looked up at me once again. For a moment, I ignored the heaviness inside me and gave her a smile. She must have sensed my effort because she nodded.

I straightened my skirt and knelt beside Camila. I helped make more vines, more paper flowers, and more talk, but this time, I listened. And slowly, one by one, the grasshoppers quit jumping.

twenty-four

CANDLELIGHT AND MARIGOLDS

Daylight faded, and the closer we got to the cemetery, the more crowded the streets grew. People carried baskets full of offerings that included paper wreaths and flowers and favorite foods of their deceased. Those who weren't strong enough to carry baskets, like the children and elderly, held burning candles that turned our dark path into a soft stream of amber light.

Camila and I walked side by side. I carried Luisito on my back while holding the crib over my left hip. Camila carried the baskets, and not too far behind us were Abuelita, Amelia, and Nina. Each of them held a lit candle with one hand and used the other to protect it from the breeze.

We followed the crowd and walked past the high stone wall that surrounded the cemetery, and as we reached the entrance, the crowd merged. A breeze swept over us, carrying smells of food, flowers, and burned wax. Before long, we entered through a wide gate beneath an iron arch that people said marked the cemetery's name—*Cementerio de San Fernando*.

Hundreds of tiny candle flames danced in the autumn breeze, illuminating the earth mounds that appeared to overlap one another in the crowded cemetery. Most graves showed the affection of people coming together with their deceased. Their wooden crosses had been dusted, straightened, and decorated with trinkets and wreaths of yellow and red paper flowers. Some mounds were covered with a blanket of flowers and outlined with bright candles.

Camila led us toward the back of the cemetery before pausing and pointing.

"He's right over there," said Camila. Her soft and gentle voice reminded me of the way people talk over a sleeping baby.

We approached the tiny earth mound where Camila's son was buried. Amelia and Nina were instructed to spread marigolds over the grave while Abuelita and I helped with the placement and lighting of the candles.

Camila gently cleaned the small white cross and placed a flower wreath over it. She positioned the crib atop the mound and inside it set the trinket flask, one bowl full of orange slices and another full of crackers, and a small bottle of milk.

Each of us placed a small prayer stone at the foot of the grave, and afterward, while sharing slices of oranges, Camila told us about her son. Abuelita and Amelia also shared stories about Mama with Camila. I sat back quietly, listening to everyone until Amelia began talking about Papa.

I straightened, frowning at her. "Don't talk about Papa, Amelia."

"Why not?" Amelia asked.

"We celebrate the dead today," I said. "So let's not talk about him."

There was a long silence until Camila broke it by talking about her son. She began to tell stories that made Nina, Amelia, and Abuelita laugh so loud, I thought they'd wake the dead.

Despite Camila's animated talk and despite the beautiful glow of the candles surrounding us, I was entombed in my own dark thoughts about Papa.

twenty-five
THE NEW BOY

An hour before sunset the next day, Camila and I boarded the streetcar for work. We sat in our usual seats—mine by the window and hers by the aisle.

I stared out the window, and in the reflection, I could see Camila glancing at me.

"You've been quiet all day," she said. "Is everything all right?"

I shrugged.

"Are you upset you went to the cemetery with us last night?"

I shook my head and kept my eyes on the people walking down the street. My night had been filled with nightmares and images of Papa dying and of Mama screaming and sobbing. I didn't want to tell Camila about them.

Our walk to the stand remained silent except for the times Camila uttered a few words here and there. Lost in thought, I kept to myself until Camila stopped in her tracks. We were a stone's throw away from the stand.

"What time is it?" said Camila.

I whipped my head back to the clock on the street corner, fearing we were late.

"We're not late," I said.

"Then why is everything set up already?"

My heart pounded. "Did Doña Carmen ask us to come earlier?"

Camila shook her head as we approached the stand. Tables, benches, and chairs had already been arranged. A young boy I'd never seen before assembled the crystal glasses into pyramids.

"I better run to the back," I said to Camila. "I need to make sure we're all stocked up."

Camila nodded as she tied the apron strings behind her waist and headed straight toward Doña Carmen.

I reached the line of barrels in the back. All of them— the corn, the rice, the flour, and the beans—were full. Next, I opened the tall tin box of coffee, and it too had been topped off. Someone had already done my job.

My eyes scanned the stand, looking for Doña Carmen, and when I spotted her, I saw Camila standing in front of her. Camila shook her head repeatedly and motioned with her arms, pointing at herself, as if she were trying to convince the queen of something. Doña Carmen stood firm with her arms crossed. The look on her face was of annoyance.

I'd seen that look before. She often gave it when she was terminating someone. My heart sank. Was the queen dismissing Camila?

I rushed toward them, hoping to change Doña Carmen's mind in time. I was sure Doña Carmen would listen to me.

Doña Carmen noticed me and motioned her head to let Camila know I was approaching.

Camila turned to me. Her face was pale and worrisome. I could tell she wanted to say something.

"What's wrong?" I asked.

Camila pursed her lips, but before she could speak, Doña Carmen snapped at her, "Camila, go do as I say, or you'll be next."

Camila shut her eyes for a moment and swallowed hard. She glanced at Doña Carmen and then at me before walking away. My eyes followed her as she reached a group of customers who had just seated themselves.

I looked at Doña Carmen. "What do you mean she'll be next?"

"Petra," said Doña Carmen, but before speaking any further, she reached into her apron, pulled out a cigarette, and lit it. She took a long drag while observing me. After releasing a cloud of smoke to the side, she said, "I won't be needing you anymore."

Her words dropped on my head like a bolt of thunder. My eyes glanced at the stand, the storefronts, at the darkening sky, and at the people placing their food orders with Camila. I wanted to convince myself that I'd misunderstood. "You mean you don't need me to run any more errands, right? Or take orders from customers?"

Doña Carmen shook her head, puffing her cigarette once more. "You're done working for me. I no longer need you."

My arms, my shoulders, my whole body grew numb as her words sank into my head.

"But...but..." My thoughts scrambled with the noises

around me—streetcar bells, honking automobiles, and laughing patrons. This couldn't be happening.

I took a step closer to Doña Carmen. "Is it because of last night? Because I wasn't here to help you?"

Doña Carmen rolled her eyes. She threw her cigarette to the ground and put her foot over it, almost stomping it. "I don't care what you do on your days off. Had you shown up yesterday, you would've been let go a day earlier."

My thoughts went to the day I'd almost lost her money. Had Don Lalo told her about it? Did she no longer trust me? "Is it because of the day I almost lost your money?"

The chili queen gave me a baffled look then seemed to recall something. "Now that you mention it..." She straightened her shoulders and lifted her chin. "I don't trust you anymore."

"But I found your money," I blurted out. "And if I hadn't, I would have found a way to replace it. I wasn't trying to steal from you." I fought back tears, knowing full well crying in front of the queen would make things worse.

A boy approached us. It was the same boy I'd seen earlier setting up the glasses. "Anything else, ma'am?"

Doña Carmen reached for her handkerchief and handed him a few coins. "Go run the errand I told you about."

The boy nodded, took the coins, and sped away.

My ears buzzed, and my face burned. "I was loyal to you."

Doña Carmen remained silent; her eyes swept across the stand.

"You said you'd take care of me if I was loyal, and I worked hard to prove it. I showed up before my shift and stayed well after it was over—I even came to work on my days off. Was that not enough?"

Doña Carmen didn't speak nor look at me. Instead, she lit another cigarette, and it took everything within to keep from slapping it away.

After a few drags, she finally spoke. "You're a hard worker, Petra, but this boy here"—the chili queen used her chin to point in the boy's direction—"he's thirteen and can carry a lot more weight than you. He's taller, stronger, and he set up this whole place in half the time it takes you. He's also the son of a friend."

"Please, Doña Carmen. I need this job."

"You said your grandmother and sister shell pecans. Join them."

"Shelling doesn't pay much," I said, moving in front of Doña Carmen as she stared at her stand. "Perhaps I can stay here and help you with something else. You could even pay me less."

Doña Carmen looked annoyed as she leaned on to one side to keep her eyes on the stand. "I don't do charity."

"Doña Carmen, my wages from the Haymarket aren't enough. I...I..." My mind raced, thinking of ways to convince Doña Carmen to keep me.

"My sister was here last night," Doña Carmen said, taking another drag of her cigarette. "She too decided to replace you with the boy at the Haymarket."

I stood motionless. The tears that had been clinging to my eyes had finally let loose and burned down my cheeks. I clenched my hands and felt my nails dig into my palms. The chili queen continued to talk, but not everything she said made it to my ears. The bits and pieces I did hear were about how hard of a worker I was but that the boy was stronger and knew how to read.

"Doña Carmen," a girl working the tables shouted. "*El Güero*, the cowboy, wants to talk to you."

"Tell him I'm on my way," Doña Carmen said.

Before walking away, the queen threw the cigarette to the ground, stepped on it, and turned to me one last time. "You'll find something soon. I have no doubt." As she walked away, she laughed, clapped her hands, and extended her arms to the cowboy making his weekly visit to the queen.

Every fiber in me wanted to scream. I wanted to run through the stand, flip over every table, and hear every crystal glass shatter. I had been a fool, and that angered me to no end. But what enraged me the most, for the first time in my life, was that I hadn't been born a boy.

twenty-six
SINGING BELLS

I darted down the main street like a raging bull. I bumped into tourists, cowboys, and soldiers who leisurely strolled the streets. Their smiles, their laughter, and even their chivalry as they moved out of the way or tipped their hats seemed like a mockery of my pain.

I dashed across streets and whisked around corners. Things that'd always fascinated me about the city—glowing signs, window displays, and band music flowing from terraces—became a blur. My legs burned, and I continued to run as fast as I could until my heart forced me to stop.

I grabbed on to a tall iron post at the end of a bridge. I hunched over it, coughing and struggling to catch my breath.

As my breathing settled, I straightened and looked around. I had no idea where I was, but the river in front of me had to be the same one that cut through the town's center.

I made my way to the middle of the bridge and stepped up on the rail's bottom edge. Dark shadows waved across the river's surface, and high above the cypress trees, a breeze began to form. It shook the treetops, undecided as to which way to go.

Images of Ehecatl—the god of wind—came to me. Abuelita had told me that long, long ago our world had once been destroyed. Ehecatl, with his long, feathered body, had entered our fallen world and grown upset when he witnessed the destruction. In his anger, he twisted his serpentlike figure, and out of his beak erupted powerful winds that swept our world clean, restoring all order back to it.

My world was falling apart, and I wondered if *Ehecatl* could restore it.

The wind grew stronger, and as it dropped from the treetops, I grabbed the rail and lifted my chin. With my eyes shut, I took in a breath of *Ehecatl's* power and wished for healing.

The strong breeze rushed through me. It brushed my face and blew back loose strands of hair. As it pushed harder against my shoulders, I increased my grip.

The wind quieted, and I opened my eyes. Nothing had been carried away or restored. My insides were still knotted, and I still didn't know where my next job was coming from. Something else came to mind, though. Something I could fix right away.

My fingers moved briskly, unlacing my shoes. I'd worn these since my first day when I searched for a place to live. I was miserable wearing them, but the nuns had assured me shoes would help me get and keep a job.

I removed one shoe and stretched my toes in relief. The real satisfaction came when I pulled my hand back and, with all my strength, tossed the shoe into the river. The second shoe, I threw so hard, I thought my arm would go along with it. My heart grew lighter, and my toes wiggled and curled as I watched the pair float down the river.

My eyes turned to a building next to the bridge. In the dim light, I made it out to be a church.

Camila had warned me that there were different Catholic churches for different people in the city. There was one was for the Irish, one for the Germans, another for the Italians, and one for the Mexicans. She had been told it was frowned upon if you walked into the wrong church.

I didn't believe it. How could the house of God be open to certain people only? In Mexico, the front pews were reserved for the rich, but the church itself was open to everyone.

I pulled the large wooden door open and let myself in.

Right at the entrance was a small basin filled with holy water. I wet the tip of my fingers, and as I began crossing myself, I stopped. My eyes opened wide as I tried to take in my surroundings.

Most churches I'd seen in my life, even the big San Fernando Cathedral we'd attended here in San Antonio, were humble in their appearance. This church was the most beautiful one I'd ever seen. The high, curved ceiling was painted with colorful shapes that formed crosses in overlapping patterns. Tall arches and columns trimmed with gold divided the wide open space of the chapel, while chandeliers filled it with soft light. The numerous stained-glass windows depicting stories from the Bible amazed me the most.

I walked toward the altar, passing rows upon rows of smooth, polished pews, all of them empty. Since no one was around to tell me where to sit, I led myself to a pew near the altar.

I had no shawl to cover my head nor rosary beads to hold. Instead, I untied my purple scarf and lifted it over my head, making me feel less exposed. I then pulled out my black rock and secured it between my clasped hands.

Kneeling, I looked in front of me. The ivory white of the altar rail and communion table matched the pureness of the Virgin Mary who sat high on top. I stared at the altar, and in the silence, my need to scream and flip tables was replaced by an urge to cry.

I was afraid to go home and tell Abuelita and Amelia I no longer had work. The rent was due in three days. There were also Abuelita's medicines and Luisito's milk. I shut my eyes and rested my head over my locked fingers. I had to think of a way out. I began to pray, not for a sign but for a way to find work.

My head was bowed when I began to hear a low

murmur. I glanced around me as it grew louder. It was a soft sound, like a chant, and it came from the front of the church.

My heart stirred. I stood up and took gentle steps toward the altar and realized the sound came from a small, open side door. I stepped through it and entered a dark, narrow hallway. Cautiously, I followed the chant down the half-lit passage.

The melody grew louder. It echoed inside the hall and within my chest. I couldn't make out the words being sung, but the voices carrying the chant sounded like bells, and every time the singing went high, goose bumps crept over the back of my head and down my arms.

I turned a corner, and at the end of the hallway was a door with light and sound pouring through. My black rock felt damp in my hand, and as I peeked into the bright room, I squeezed it tight, anticipating a chorus of angels.

At the far end of the large room, a choir of young boys stood on risers and sang. Most had blond and brown hair, and a few had hair as red as Mr. Bob's. A nun stood tall in front of them, motioning her fingers to the rhythm of the chant. She wore a black habit like the nuns at the Wesley House.

The singing grew more powerful. I had been trying to remain hidden in the dark corridor, but in my distraction, I had stepped completely inside the room without anyone noticing. My eyes fluttered and dampened as the sound grew more intense.

Suddenly the singing came to a halt. A thick silence fell upon the entire room.

I hadn't been seen, and slowly, I stepped back, hoping not to be noticed, when my black rock slipped out of my hand and hit the tile floor.

Clank!

Instantly, all eyes were on me.

I froze. I couldn't move.

One boy pointed at me. He shouted something in English, and the whole choir broke into laughter.

My heart pounded through my ears. I trembled as Camila's warning about not all churches being for Mexicans came to me.

The nun shouted and clapped her hands at the boys. As they quieted down, she turned to me. I made a swift move to pick up my rock, but in my attempt, my big toe got ahead of me and kicked it. The rock skidded across the floor and disappeared under an enormous cabinet. My heart dropped.

A wave of laughs and giggles followed.

I ran to the cabinet, dropped to my knees, and placed my head on the floor. My eyes scanned for the rock under the dusty shadows of the furniture. Behind me, I could hear the nun clapping away at the boys.

I spotted my rock and stretched my arm as far as it would go. Unable to reach it, I looked up and saw the nun talking to the boys, who'd begun to settle.

I repositioned myself, but with every stretch of my arm, my fingertips pushed the rock farther and farther away.

I looked up again, and this time, the nun marched toward me, her deep-blue eyes narrowing. I shot up, and my legs reacted on their own, bolting me back into the hallway, past the altar, and through the chapel. I pushed open the heavy door and ran back into the darkness.

twenty-seven

NUTS, SHOES, AND NUNS

My world seemed to have turned upside down after I lost my job with the chili queen. Almost a week had gone by, and work was nowhere to be found. Just as hopeless were my attempts to rescue my baby diamond from the church. Only one good thing had happened: another visit from my cousin Pablo.

He had shown up in the middle of a cool, rainy evening. We all sat near the stove, wide-eyed, listening to his stories about how trains worked and how he was learning to fix them. He used his humor and charm to tell us about his travels and made it sound like they were all great adventures. Amelia begged for more stories, but despite the different questions she'd ask, Pablo kept his memories of the revolution to himself.

"But Pablo," Amelia insisted. "How did you get here from Mexico?"

Pablo paused, thought for a moment, then smiled. "Ehecatl got me here."

"Ehecatl?" Amelia looked puzzled. "The god of wind?"

Pablo nodded. "It was midday. I was working the fields when everything went dark. I looked up, searching for the sun, and over the mountains was the biggest storm I'd ever seen."

Amelia squeezed her arms around her knees, curling herself around them. Even Luisito sat quietly on Pablo's lap.

"Dark, scary clouds swirled over the mountaintops," Pablo continued, "and the sky roared with thick lightning bolts firing across the desert. Some almost reached me. But you know what?"

"What?" Amelia said.

"Despite all the fussing and rumbling of the sky," Pablo smiled. "It didn't rain. Not a single drop. Instead, the whirl of clouds uncoiled and stretched out like an angry serpent ready to strike. And right before my eyes, the whole storm turned into giant wind gust that slithered down the mountain toward me."

"What did you do?" asked Amelia.

"I pressed down on my sombrero and ran as fast as I could, but the wind was so powerful, it caught up with me and lifted me into the sky. I was scared, but when I realized it was Ehecatl who carried me, I relaxed. I glided like a bird over the desert." Pablo made whistling sounds and moved his hand to show us how he glided. "I saw canyons and then flew over a long, silver ribbon that weaved across the desert—it was el Río Bravo."

Amelia's eyes sparkled as she turned to Nina in awe. Her wide smile revealed the gap of her two front missing teeth.

Before leaving, Pablo gave Abuelita some money. He offered me some, but I refused to take it.

"You are one big mule, prima," Pablo said. "But lucky for you, a mule in America goes a lot further than one in Mexico."

I rolled my eyes at his words and hugged him goodbye.

My mornings now consisted of going with Amelia to the nearby creek to gather pecans. Amelia led the way every day, skipping, excited to show me over and over the best pecan trees lining the San Pedro Creek. In a little over an hour, we'd fill three small gunnysacks with pecans. This was a lot more than the usual single sack Amelia could fill by herself in three hours.

Afterward, we'd rush home, and together with Abuelita, we'd sit at the table and shell as many pecans as we could while Nina played with Luisito. But no matter how fast we'd crack, open, and extract the nut-meat, three hours of shelling added up to only three pounds of shelled pecans and a room full of air that made your throat scratchy. Amelia and Nina would then take the large pecan-filled canister to the bakery and sell the nuts for about twenty-five or thirty cents.

For lunch, Abuelita would take the children to the Wesley House soup kitchen. She'd insist that I go too for a bowl of soup or to ask the nuns about work. I'd always turn down her offer and say that I wasn't hungry, that my chances of finding work on my own were better. I hadn't mentioned to Abuelita anything about my brush with the angry nun or my fear of coming across her at the Wesley House.

In the afternoons, I'd go downtown to continue my search for work. Store or restaurant owners would turn me down with either a sad smile or a frown at my bare feet. Once darkness fell, I'd make my way to the church where I'd lost my rock.

First, I'd stop at the bridge and spy on the entrance from there. If no one went in or came out, I'd move a little closer. There were a few times I'd made it all the way inside, but it never worked. There'd always be at least one person at the pews. I couldn't take my chances, so I'd walk away and wait for another time.

Early one morning down by the creek, sunlight filtered through the leaves of the tall pecan trees. Their majestic branches, holding clusters upon clusters of ripe pecans, swayed in the cool autumn breeze. From the ground, I could see the husks, which had once been green but now carried the same gray color as the shacks we lived in. Each of those husks had encased a pecan in total darkness, waiting for the perfect time to open and release its earthen scent into the air. Each had withered beautifully by splitting at the seams and curling back to reveal the new life within.

I followed Amelia down to the grassy bank where patches of dew dampened my bare feet. Amelia reached the edge of the creek and, before crossing it, turned back to me. "Ready to cross?"

I nodded, rubbing the chill away from my arms.

Seven large rocks lay across the creek and formed a passage to the other side. Amelia hopped from rock to rock and chanted, "*Uno, dos, tres, yo quiero mucha nuez.*"

"Why do you say you want lots of pecans every time you cross?" I asked.

"For good luck," Amelia said. "Every time I say it, I find a lot of pecans on that side of the creek."

"Why won't you say it coming back? That way you'd find lots of pecans on this side too."

"I tried, but it didn't work," Amelia said.

"It didn't work because that side of the creek has more trees."

Amelia shrugged, looking at the treetops above her. "Maybe. But I also think the pecans on this side are bigger too. Besides, I like saying it because *nuez* and *tres* rhyme."

I followed Amelia's footsteps over the rocks, not hopping but rather stretching my arms out to steady myself.

The stones broke the gentle rhythm of the stream, creating soft gurgling sounds as cool water splashed at my feet.

"You should mind these rocks every time you cross," I said. "They're slippery."

"That's why I hop, so I don't slip."

Strong gusts set in as we gathered pecans. They sent ripples across the creek and made our eyes squint. At times, they shook the treetops so much, it appeared to be raining pecans. Amelia and I hurried to pick them up before the squirrels could get to them first.

The wind also chilled me, especially when it swept across my wet feet. I tried warming them up by rubbing them with my hands, but it didn't seem to help.

"How did you lose your shoes?" Amelia asked.

"I told you, already. Ehecatl took them."

Amelia pulled her chin down and scowled. "Why would the god of wind take your shoes? Gods don't wear shoes, especially Ehecatl."

"Do you believe Ehecatl carried Pablo across the Río Grande?"

"I do."

"Then why can't you believe he took my shoes?"

"Because Abuelita says Ehecatl fixes things. He carried Pablo to America to fix things in his life."

"Well, maybe Ehecatl wanted to help fix the blisters and calluses on my feet."

Amelia shook her head and gave a small sigh. She picked a few more pecans then stopped.

"You know what I think?" Amelia smirked and crossed her arms. "Ehecatl didn't take your shoes. You threw them away."

"That's silly," I said, turning away and feeling my face grow hot. "And even if I did, that's none of your concern. Now keep picking before we run out of time."

"The Wesley House is having a party today," said Amelia as she gathered more pecans. "Abuelita says they're giving lots of things away: coats, blankets... shoes."

Amelia emphasized the word *shoes*, and I rolled my eyes.

"They're even having a piñata." Amelia paused. "Maybe you can come with us."

I shook my head. "Can't go. I have to find work."

"But Abuelita says the nuns there can help you."

I stopped picking nuts and turned to Amelia.

"Do you know all the nuns at the Wesley House?"

Amelia inspected one of the pecans she'd picked. "I think I do. Especially the ones that give away candy. Why?"

"Have any of them said anything to you about me? Maybe yesterday or in the past few days when you all went there for soup?"

Amelia scrunched her lips to the side and glanced up. "No. I don't think so."

"Do you know a nun who has deep-blue eyes?"

Amelia squeezed her lips again. "A lot of them have blue eyes."

"I mean really blue. As blue as the lake back in Esperanzas."

"Yes." Amelia jumped. "Sister Nora. She's got *really* blue eyes."

"Do you see Sister Nora a lot? Is she nice?"

"She never gives out candy, but she's a little nice. I didn't see her yesterday or the day before. I think the last time I saw her was—" Amelia stopped. Her eyes widened. "Are you in trouble, Petra? Is that why you haven't gone to the Wesley House?" She glanced at my feet and gasped, her face twice as horrified. "Is that how you lost your shoes? You threw them at Sister Nora?"

"No. That's nonsense."

"Then what happened to your shoes? And why don't you want to go to the Wesley House, even for soup?"

"Never mind. I shouldn't have said anything. Finish up. We have to go."

Amelia continued gathering pecans, but all the while, she kept her eyes on me and on my bare feet.

I snapped at her, "Will you stop staring at my feet?"

Amelia pursed her lips and grabbed a few more pecans before peeking into her gunnysack. "I'm ready."

I looked inside my gunnysack. It too was full.

"Petra," Amelia said.

"What?"

"If you really aren't in trouble, come to the party with us."

I was cornered. If I didn't go, Amelia would tell Abuelita about her suspicions, and if Abuelita believed, even for the slightest moment, that I'd flung my shoes at a nun, she'd kill me.

"Fine," I said. "I'll go."

twenty-eight
SUNFLOWERS & COPPER

By midafternoon, the wind had settled, and the sun's warmth poured over us as we stood and watched automobiles of every color drive around the streets near the Wesley House. It was a parade the nuns had organized to raise money for their cause. The automobiles' roaring engines and loud honks brought smiles to neighborhood children sitting on the sidewalks.

After the parade was over, we followed the stream of people to the Wesley House. Amelia, Nina, and I remained outside and approached tables filled with cookies and tiny pastries. A small band sitting near the tables began to play.

All sorts of people mingled and walked in and out of the house. Most were like us, from Los Corrales, but the people who stood out were the ones who had been riding in the automobiles. The men were dressed in smooth dark suits and the women, as elegant as storefront mannequins, wore feathered or flowered hats and long, straight silk skirts, some embroidered with tiny flowers. Unlike the rich Mexicans I came across back home at the plaza in Esperanzas, these wealthy Anglos made eye contact with me, most smiled at me, and some even greeted me. They were the ones donating money to the Wesley House.

Amelia and Nina nibbled on cookies and watched the band play while my eyes darted from the front door to the gate entrance. My heart raced, hoping I wouldn't see the blue-eyed nun, Sister Nora. I held one cookie inside a folded napkin, but by now it had crumbled into a million pieces.

Finally, we went inside to join Abuelita and Camila. All the furniture inside the Wesley House had been pushed against the walls, and tables in the center of the rooms held mountains of clothes and blankets for us to pick out.

"Take Amelia to the next room," Abuelita said, "and pick a coat."

I was relieved when I didn't see a nun in the hallway nor in the room with the coats.

Nina, Amelia, and I stood at the tables, sorting through stacks of coats. As I combed through a large pile I came across a yellow sleeve. I tugged on it hard but was careful enough not to rip it or cause an avalanche. And out of the heap of dark wool came out the most beautiful coat I'd ever seen.

I stroked its collar and its large copper buttons, each designed as a sunflower. The coat's yellow fabric was as bright as the summer sun and as warm as the month of May. I flipped it around, grabbed it by the shoulder seams, and measured it over me. It seemed to be my size.

"That's a beautiful coat," said Amelia.

"It has a small stain here," I said, pointing to the bottom near the hem, "and a missing button, but it fits well."

"You think we can find one my size?" Amelia asked, sweeping each button with her hand.

"Have you searched though the small coats already?" I asked.

"We did," said Amelia, "but only saw brown and gray coats."

It then dawned on me. Yellow was Amelia's favorite color.

"Amelia," Abuelita shouted from the other room. "*Ven p'acá.*"

"Go see what Abuelita wants," I said, "and I'll search this big coat pile. Maybe I'll find another yellow one."

Amelia and Nina left the room, and once again I dug into the large pile of coats in front of me. I came across dark blue coats, brown coats, and lots of gray coats that looked as sad as the shacks we lived in. There was no other yellow coat in sight.

Suddenly, something outside the window caught my eye.

A group of nuns had gathered in a circle just a few steps from the window. The one with her back toward me seemed to be sharing a story. She motioned her arms up and down while the rest of the nuns looked at her in shock. A few of them shook their heads, two held a hand over their mouths, and one of them crossed herself almost nonstop. It had to be Sister Nora, who had gathered all the nuns to warn them about me.

"Petra," Amelia whispered. She tugged at my skirt.

"Not now, Amelia." I said, keeping my eyes on the nuns, hoping the one talking would turn around.

"Petra." Amelia's voice grew more pressing. She pulled at my skirt with urgency.

I turned to her, and through clenched teeth, I said, "Amelia, can't you just—"

I suddenly went stiff. Behind Amelia stood the nun with the fierce blue eyes.

Sister Nora.

twenty-nine
NEW SHOES

"**Buenos días, Petra,**" said Sister Nora with half a smile.

I swallowed hard; the nun knew my name already. I turned to Amelia, wondering if she had told her my name. Or had Amelia come to warn me about her?

Sister Nora stooped down to Amelia. "M'ija, *corriste hecha la cochinilla.* Why did you run so fast when I called for you?"

Amelia was speechless. She hid her face behind my skirt.

There was something about the way Sister Nora pronounced her words. She spoke Spanish without an American accent and spoke it like me and like Abuelita.

Sister Nora straightened and introduced herself to me. "I have something for you."

Amelia's head popped from behind me. "Is it Petra's shoes?"

Sister Nora gave her a confused look, and when she noticed my bare feet, she chuckled. "No, no shoes, but we can certainly find some later."

Sister Nora reached into the pocket of her robe, and Amelia, still holding at my skirt, stretched her neck, wanting to see what Sister Nora was pulling out.

Sister Nora uncurled her fingers, and in the middle of her palm was my baby diamond.

"You left this at my church last week," Sister Nora said.

Amelia gasped. "Petra, it's your rock."

"Thank you," I said and grabbed it.

"That's Petra's favorite rock," said Amelia. "It looks small and boring, but it's really a—"

"Amelia, shh," I said, hushing her.

Sister Nora pressed her lips into a thin line, as if trying to hide a big smile that still shone through her eyes.

"That's a beautiful coat you've got there," Sister Nora said.

"It is pretty," said Amelia. "The buttons look like flowers."

"They do," said Sister Nora before turning to me. "Does it fit?"

Amelia's face beamed. "It does. Put it on, Petra, so Sister Nora can see you."

"Actually," I said. "I think it's a little big."

Amelia looked confused, but when I stooped down and measured the coat against her body, her mouth dropped open as if she'd seen a shooting star.

"It's for me?" said Amelia. "But it doesn't fit."

"We'll roll up the sleeves," I said. "And maybe after I buy some yellow thread, I can raise the hem—"

"May I?" Sister Nora extended her arm for the coat.

I handed the coat to her, and she held it out and glanced at Amelia. She pulled a pair of spectacles from her pocket, set them over her eyes, and inspected the stitching.

"Come to my church tomorrow," Sister Nora said, handing back the coat. "Bring the coat and one of Amelia's dresses, and I'll show you how to alter it."

The chance to learn something new excited me, but I remembered Camila's words about Mexicans not being allowed in a church like Sister Nora's. I wanted to ask if that was true, but I couldn't bring myself to speak.

"You look worried," said Sister Nora. "Do you work tomorrow? If so, you can come afterward."

"Petra doesn't have a job anymore," Amelia said.

"What happened?" Sister Nora asked. "Did the chili queen let you go?"

I nodded and wondered how much Sister Nora knew about me.

"If that's the case, come to my church early tomorrow morning," Sister Nora said. "We could use some help around the church."

"What about Petra's shoes?" said Amelia.

I shot a stare at Amelia. We had bothered Sister Nora enough.

"That's right." Sister Nora gave Amelia a wink.

We followed Sister Nora down the hallway and into another room. Sister Nora was a tall woman. She was about two heads taller than me, and despite looking as old and wrinkly as Abuelita, she had solid shoulders and her steps were strong and swift like a soldier's.

"Take these." Sister Nora handed me several pairs of stockings before standing right beside me. She lifted her cloak enough to expose her foot and lined it up next to mine.

"You're small," said Sister Nora, "but your feet are almost as big as mine." She handed me a pair of laced boots. "Try these."

I sighed. The thought of squeezing my feet into another pair of leather clamps made my feet throb.

"Put the stockings on first," said Sister Nora.

I dusted my feet, put the stockings on, and, as if by magic, my feet slipped smoothly into the shoes. I felt as if I were wearing nothing.

"What's wrong?" said Sister Nora. "Are they too tight?"

I shook my head. "I thought all shoes were supposed to hurt."

"Mine don't hurt," said Amelia.

"Things that fit well shouldn't cause pain," said Sister Nora.

I looked at my new shoes and wondered if it was the stockings or the shoe size that had made the difference.

"I'll see you tomorrow, Petra," said Sister Nora, "and give my best to your grandmother and Camila."

I nodded, and after Sister Nora walked out of the room, Amelia ran to me and hugged me.

"You found your baby diamond, Petra. You also got new shoes and a new job. Let's go tell Abuelita."

"Amelia, I don't know if I have a job, yet. Sister Nora only said she needed help."

"Abuelita always says, '*Algo es algo.*'"

That was true. Something was better than nothing, and right now all I could do was take what I could get and hope that something better came along.

thirty

CRISSCROSSED WRINKLES

Morning light poured over the church's courtyard and into Sister Nora's room. She and the other nuns lived in a wing across the courtyard from the boys' grammar school building.

Sister Nora stood by the window and rummaged through a tin box filled with spools, pincushions, and scraps of fabric. She had spectacles on and hummed the tune I'd heard the choirboys sing. I sat nearby on a small bed pushed to a corner. Spread next to me on the bed were Amelia's dress and the yellow coat.

The walls of Sister Nora's room were the color of a cloudy sky, bare except for a wooden crucifix hanging over the head of her bed. Across from me were a small table and two mismatched chairs. Near the door to my right was a strange table with iron extensions on the bottom, and to my left was an old cabinet with a small clock on top. I gasped when my gaze dropped to the two shelves filled with at least ten or so books. It was the most books I'd seen in my entire life.

"There it is." Sister Nora held up a little gadget in her hand, and she pulled a long ribbon out of it. She called it a tape and used it to measure Amelia's dress. She scribbled away numbers on a piece of paper and glanced at the clock.

"Can you leave Amelia's dress and the coat with me overnight?"

I nodded.

"I was hoping to teach you how to use the sewing machine"—Sister Nora glanced at the clock once more—"but I have a big meal to prepare for a group coming from Mexico whom Father Amaro wants to welcome."

"Refugees?"

"No. They're more like political exiles escaping the war."

I didn't know what political exiles were, but if they were running from the same nightmare I had fled, my heart went out to them.

"Father Amaro always enjoys having them as dinner guests," Sister Nora said. "He says it reminds him of his dinners back in Mexico City."

Suddenly I had an idea. "Would it be okay if I helped you with the meal? I can help you serve too. I learned how when I worked for the chili queen." I hoped Sister Nora said yes. I wanted to help make these people fleeing the war feel welcomed.

Sister Nora's face lit up. "That'd be wonderful."

The church's kitchen was much bigger than the shack I lived in. Above the massive center table hung a collection of shiny copper pots and pans, and the shelves and cabinets held all sorts of cookware. Tall pieces of furniture Sister Nora referred to as cupboards were filled with delicate cups, dishes, and bowls. There were two sinks, two gas ranges, four ovens, and something called an icebox that helped keep the food cold.

The pantry looked big enough to hold ten people. I helped Sister Nora gather the flour, sugar, and other powders and spices with names I didn't know. She took out things I had never seen before: an eggbeater, a sifter, and my favorite, a rolling pin. It was as if I had stepped into another world.

"Have you had apple pie before?" asked Sister Nora.

"No, ma'am," I said, as scents of cinnamon and brown sugar from the apple mixture filled my nostrils. I poured the last batch into the fifth and final pie.

"It's a favorite here in America," she said. "I'm curious to see if you'll like it."

I rolled out the last batch of dough and wondered why Americans cooked so different from us.

"Why do you have to measure everything?" I asked. "My grandmother never measures things when she cooks."

"Sure she does," said Sister Nora. "When I cook tamales or *mole*, I measure things using my hands, my fingers, and even my eyes."

I stopped rolling the pin. "Where did you learn to cook mole and tamales? And your Spanish." I chuckled. "You speak it like me."

Sister Nora smiled like I had complimented her. "I lived two years in Mexico."

"Did you live in a church?"

"No, I volunteered as a nurse for *La Cruz Blanca*, the White Cross. I treated rebel soldiers and got to spend lots of time with soldaderas."

My mind went to the soldaderas, Doña Amparo, Luz, and Luz's baby, Chencha, whom I'd met at the rebel military camp on our way to the border. Unlike Marietta, the rebel who only worked and trained as a soldier, soldaderas were the brave women who followed husbands, sons, and fathers into the revolution to watch after them. They cooked for them, washed their clothes, and never hesitated to pick up a weapon and fight in the trenches while their men ate.

"Mexico is a beautiful country," Sister Nora continued. "I fell in love with its people. I didn't want to leave them, but when I learned about all the refugee children coming to San Antonio, I couldn't wait to get back."

I finished rolling out the crust, placed it over the last pie, and sealed it.

"Did I flute the edges correctly?" I asked Sister Nora.

She inspected the pie with a smile hidden behind thinly pressed lips. The lamp above shed warm light over the small brown spots that dwelled on the aged skin of her face. Her skin was worn and had wrinkles on top of wrinkles that crisscrossed each other, but her button nose resembled that of the porcelain doll's I'd seen in a display window, and the pink glow on her cheeks made her blue eyes as bright as could be.

I couldn't tell how old Sister Nora was, but she was beautiful.

Sister Nora and I placed the pies in the oven, and as we cleaned up, she talked about her work at the church.

"The rugs need cleaning, the floors need scrubbing, and there's lots of dusting to do. If you agree to help me, we can start our mornings shopping, followed by cleaning, cooking, and more cleaning. Depending on how many dinner guests we have, we may have more to do."

Sister Nora spoke fast, but I liked how she said *we*.

"Does six dollars a week sound alright to you?" she asked.

I was confused. "Six dollars for shopping?"

"No, I meant paying you six dollars a week for helping me. Is that alright?"

I felt like I was about to burst with excitement. The most I'd ever made with the chili queen and the Haymarket combined was five dollars a week. I fought hard to contain myself and make sure I'd understood correctly.

"You're paying me six dollars to help you clean, cook, *and* shop?"

"It'll be for six days of work, about seven to eight hours each day, sometimes ten, depending on what's happening at the church. Is that fine?"

I tried pressing my lips together, but my mouth still felt loose and shaky. "Yes," I said, nodding repeatedly. "It's...fine."

"Very well," said Sister Nora. "Let's get to work."

A frenzy of thoughts fired through my mind. I'd be able to restart our savings and start thinking of ways to find Papa once again.

A sudden dread put a halt to everything. What if someone bigger or stronger came along and took this job? What if someone who knew how to read took it away?

I tried to ignore this feeling as Sister Nora showed me how to use things like the meat grinder, the vacuum cleaner, and the power washer—a machine that could wash a load of clothes in less than ten minutes. I operated each machine, shooting glances at Sister Nora, and with every nod or wink she gave, her smiling eyes assured me I was doing things right.

Like Doña Carmen, Sister Nora had a strong, commanding stance. Unlike the chili queen, though, I could tell Sister Nora had a kinder, much nobler heart, and I could feel my dread ebbing away.

thirty-one
LITTLE ROSE

I had never learned so much in my entire life than in the twenty days I'd been working for Sister Nora. At the end of each workday, it was my mind that was exhausted, more so than my body.

Early on I had expressed my desire to learn to read, and immediately, Sister Nora took it on as a challenge for both of us. Before teaching me my first letter, she said something I knew I'd never to forget: "There's great power in the written word."

"That's why things like books, signs, and contracts carry so much power," she added. "Spoken words are like old winter leaves—they're easily spun, blown away, and forgotten."

"So written words are better than spoken ones?" I'd asked one morning as we shopped.

"Both are good, but it's easier to interrupt or silence a spoken word."

Sister Nora had begun teaching me three letters a day. While cooking she'd ask me to use my finger to scribble them over the flour-covered baking sheet, and when we shopped, she'd call them out and had me find them on street signs or storefronts. I was now recognizing grocer names like C.C. Butt and words like *farmacia*, pharmacy, and *apotheke*. Later I came to learn that Sister Nora had been teaching me to read words in Spanish, English, and German.

Sometimes, while cooking or cleaning, Sister Nora spoke to me in English or German. At first, I panicked because I didn't understand any of it.

"Don't trouble yourself," Sister Nora would say after having switched to Spanish. "Just listen. You learn a language with your ears first, then your tongue, and at the end, it's your brain that puts it all together." She said that was the way babies learned to talk.

Sister Nora and I had begun our morning shopping one day with a stop at the Haymarket followed by a trip to the butcher.

"Did you like living in Mexico despite the war?" I said, grabbing a bundle of meat off the counter. I nodded and gave Herr Schmidt, the German butcher, a smile. He returned the smile and nodded as Sister Nora paid him and thanked him in German.

"I loved living in Mexico" Sister Nora said. "I loved the food, the culture—it reminded me a lot of my own."

"Your American culture?"

"No." Sister Nora chuckled as we stepped onto the crowded sidewalk. "I'm Irish. Well, I'm American now, but I'm originally from Ireland."

"Where's that?"

"Ireland is in Europe. Have you heard of Europe?"

"I think I have," I said. Papa had told me that Europe was a land far away, on the other side of a big body of water. That was the place where the Spanish conquistadores had come from.

"When did you come to America?"

"Ages ago," said Sister Nora as we sidestepped pedestrians. "I was six years old, and I came here with my big sister, Róisín. She was twelve."

I beamed. "Just like Amelia and me."

"We came alone," Sister Nora added. "Our mother and

father died when I was five, and my grandmother took care of us before sending Róisín and me to America."

"Was there a revolution in Ireland? Is that why you came here?"

"No, but just as bad. It was a potato blight. Most of Ireland was a poor country. We depended on potatoes to feed our families, and one day, they all turned black. Without anything to eat, people began to starve."

Sister Nora didn't say anything more as we crossed the street. I itched to know more, though. Róisín had been my age when she came to America! I wanted to know if she'd been happy, excited, or scared when she got here. I wanted to find out if she'd found work just like me.

As we approached the iron bridge on our way back to the church, I noticed, for the first time, a sign attached to one of its pillars. It was an iron plate engraved with three distinct groups of words.

"What does that say?" I asked.

"It's an old sign," said Sister Nora, walking up to it. "It's always amused me because it's written in three different languages, yet the translation is different for all three."

Sister Nora pointed at the topmost line of words.

"This sentence is in English, and it says, 'Walk your horse over this bridge, or you will be fined.'"

Sister Nora turned to me. "That's because Americans care more about their pockets than anything else."

Her finger then moved to the sentence below. She read every German word aloud and translated the sentence. "This says, 'It is forbidden to ride fast over this bridge.'"

"That's it?" I said. "No punishment?"

Sister Nora shook her head with a grin. "No need. Germans are obsessed with following rules; it pains them not to follow an order through and through."

"The last sentence is in Spanish, right?" I asked, anxious to hear what it said.

Sister Nora nodded. "Walk your horse slowly over this bridge, or fear the law."

"*Fear* the law?" I asked. It was as if dynamite had gone off inside me. Ever since the conquest of our ancestors, fears had haunted indios and mestizos for centuries. But we were in a new country now, free to start anew. Why bring those fears across the border with us? Why not leave them in the depths of the Río Grande?

My teeth were grinding. "Why are we seen as people of fear?"

Sister Nora gave a small sigh. "M'ija, these are only generalizations, misconceptions."

We both continued to walk, but my insides churned thinking of all the people I'd met since our arrival—Mr. Bob, Don Wong, and Herr Schmidt. Did they all see me as a person of fear?

"People are lazy," said Sister Nora. "We see someone and quickly want to categorize them, like a book that hasn't been read. We keep ourselves from opening each book, reading it, and learning how unique it is."

I appreciated what Sister Nora was saying, but her words couldn't stomp out the fire inside me.

Later that afternoon when Sister Nora and I were scrubbing the floors in the choir room, images of the sign on the bridge and of the word *fear* flashed inside my head. I scrubbed harder, wishing I'd be able to scour away the notion people had of us.

Sister Nora seemed to sense my thoughts. "Don't let that sign bother you," she said. "Life's too short to dwell on things. Besides"—she paused to rinse her brush—"fear is not a bad thing when it's balanced. Fear makes you value life."

"How did you feel when you first read that sign?" I asked. "Were you upset about being fined?"

"That sign never bothered me because I've never had a horse nor money. Not to mention I'm still very close to my Irish roots."

"Do the Irish care about their pockets as much as the Americans?"

Sister Nora stopped scrubbing. "You know what the Irish care most about?"

I shook my head.

"Curses," said Sister Nora, her eyes widening. "If the sign had a sentence in Gaelic, the Irish language, it would have read, 'Walk your horse over this bridge, or be struck by lightning.' That's how you get to an Irishman—threaten him with a curse."

"I thought only Mexicans believed in curses."

Sister Nora went back to scrubbing with a wide grin. "Oh, child. The Irish and Mexicans are more similar than you think. We both believe in curses, in signs, in ghosts. For instance, we have fairy doctors, and you have *curanderas*. We have Hallowtide, you have Día de los Muertos."

Sister Nora moved her bucket closer to mine. "What does the name Cuauhtémoc mean to you?"

My heart leaped. "He's our hero," I said. "He's the Aztec warrior who sacrificed himself for his people."

Sister Nora gave a big nod. "We have our own hero too—Cú Chulainn. He did the same for the Irish."

She continued. "Breaking a mirror means terrible luck for the Irish, even death—"

"Just like breaking a metate," I said, in awe. I stopped scrubbing. "How can two different people be so much alike?"

"People are more similar than they think, but we like to convince ourselves that we're different because it makes us feel special."

"I don't believe in curses," I said. "Three years ago, a smoking star crossed our sky, and our entire village cried and prayed for mercy, saying it was the end of the world. Even my mama, who was alive then, cried too."

"You mean the comet?"

"Yes," I said. "Papa's boss from the mine called it that. But I don't believe it was bad omen or that it brought the revolution. I don't believe any of it."

Sister Nora dried the floor, and all the while she looked at me with a smirk.

"What?" I asked. "You think it's true?"

"No. I smile because you remind me of my sister, Róisín. She too believed signs and curses were all nonsense."

"Her name sounds Spanish," I said. "Is it Irish?"

"It is. It means little rose. But Róisín was far from being a small flower. She was a lion at heart."

Sister Nora went back to drying off the floor. "My sister loved to whistle, but my mother forbade her to do it because it brought bad luck."

"Whistling brought bad luck?" I asked surprised.

"Only if a girl or a woman did it," Sister Nora said, "but Róisín disagreed and whistled no matter how much it upset both my mother and grandmother. She claimed all superstitions had been created by men because it was also bad luck to ask a man where he was going fishing."

"That's silly," I said, wishing I could meet Róisín one day. "Where does Róisín live?"

Sister Nora stopped her drying, and I saw a glimpse of sadness in her eyes. "Róisín passed many, many years ago."

I wanted to ask Sister Nora more, but the quietness

that followed as we continued to work on the floor made me uneasy. I quickly began thinking of questions to ask or things to say—anything to get Sister Nora's mind off her sadness.

"How many books do you have?" I asked her.

Sister Nora looked baffled. "I, uh...probably have about ten or twelve books."

I nodded, and her eyes went back to the floor. She remained quiet, and again, my mind spun thinking of what to ask next.

A moment passed, and Sister Nora set the rag aside. She glanced toward the door before turning to me and speaking in a low voice. "I actually have a lot more books, though." She leaned toward me and used her hand to shield the side of her mouth. "They're hidden inside a chest, under my bed."

"They're hidden?" I asked in the same whisper-like voice.

Sister Nora nodded. Her eyes gleamed just like Amelia's when she's about to tell me a secret.

"Let's finish up," Sister Nora said. "And I'll show you my hidden treasure."

thirty-two

STORIES, PLANETS, AND TREASURES

I grabbed an iron handle and, inch by inch, I dragged out Sister Nora's trunk from under her bed. Dust flew into the air, giving my nose a sudden itch.

Sister Nora popped the latches open and lifted the top. She removed a top layer of folded linen, and underneath were large white paper envelopes. Each was stamped with the image of a dog looking into a large horn.

"What are those?" I asked.

"They're records. You place them on a Victrola, a talking machine, and music comes out."

"Music?" I peeked inside one of the envelopes and saw a thin black disc the size of a plate. "How?"

"I'd show you but..." Sister Nora gave a sigh, "We

don't have a Victrola here. But as soon as I come across one, I'll show you how it works."

Sister Nora continued to dig into the trunk. Beneath the records, protected by soft blankets, was a small box that held a wooden spyglass, or what she referred to as a telescope. She also pulled out two small tin boxes filled with coins from all over the world, and beneath it all, at the very bottom of the trunk, were Sister Nora's hidden books.

Her eyes glimmered with every book she pulled out. "These books," she said, "have changed the way people see themselves, the world, and the universe." She read out names I'd never heard before: Copernicus, Galileo, and Darwin. She explained what science and math were and told me about how these men had studied many things from celestial bodies to the origins of life.

"So the Earth spins like a top?" I asked. My head tingled with numbness.

"Not only does it spin, but it also moves around the sun like this." Sister Nora's finger traced a circular line that represented the Earth's path around the sun.

"How do you know so much?" I asked, feeling dizzy.

"I've read many, many books." Sister Nora patted the

stack of books next to her. "Books have taught me most of what I know."

My hand reached for a stack of books and touched the golden letters along each spine. "What about these books?" I asked.

"These books are fiction. The stories in them aren't real. They're made up."

"Can you still learn from them?"

"*Por supuesto*, m'ija," Sister Nora said. "You can learn from them just as much. Fiction books take you on adventures. Some show you human despair and resilience."

"This one is my favorite," Sister Nora said. She grabbed a thick maroon book from the stack. "It's called *The Miserable Ones*."

I thought about the title and couldn't think of anyone more miserable than the people escaping the war in Mexico.

Sister Nora handed me the book. "Take a look inside. It's illustrated. It has drawings."

This was the first time I'd ever held a book. My trembling hands cracked it open, and an ocean of words appeared in front of me.

Some of the book's black-and-white drawings portrayed a city with smoke-filled streets and bodies of soldiers lying about. Others showed people dressed in fine clothes inside cozy homes. I turned the pages but took my time when they showed poor people. I knew they were poor because of their ragged clothes and bare feet. In one drawing, a woman holding up a flag was so poor, her entire top was ripped open, exposing her chest.

One image stopped me from turning the pages. It showed a frail little girl about Amelia's age. The fear on the girl's face was one I'd seen before on Amelia and Luisito. What struck me the most was the girl's fair skin and light-colored hair.

"Who's this little girl?" I asked.

Sister Nora stretched over to see. "That's Cosette."

"Why is she barefoot? Is she poor?"

Sister Nora nodded.

"But she's white." Before Sister Nora could answer, I snickered. "I've never seen a light-skinned girl be barefoot or wear ragged clothes. They always wear silk."

"I grew up barefoot," said Sister Nora. "Róisín and I both did."

I nodded then grimaced as shame came over me.

"When I was a child, Ireland was very much like Mexico, but instead of haciendas and hacendados, we had English landlords who owned entire communities."

"Were your houses small like ours?"

"They were exactly like yours—one-room cottages made out of mud with thatched roofs."

Sister Nora went on to describe the potato blight, the day the crop they'd relied on for generations had gone bad. She said the stench of field upon field of rotting potatoes was something that would turn your stomach in the blink of an eye. Everyone had thought it was a curse, except for Róisín, of course. According to Sister Nora, she blamed everything on the English.

"My father grew oats, barley, and wheat," Sister Nora continued, "but we couldn't eat any of it because it was used to pay the English landlord for the rent. But when the potatoes kept turning to mud, Father let us eat it, and we were quickly evicted."

"Is that when you came to America?"

Sister Nora gave a heavy sigh. "No. We lived in a ditch in the woods when Mother and our infant brother died. We moved to a city afterward, and Father starved to death soon after finding work."

I crossed myself. I couldn't imagine watching my father waste away.

"I don't know who the English are," I said. "But I hate them."

"Don't," said Sister Nora. "Hate's never good. It clouds your mind and doesn't let you think straight." She placed the books back inside her trunk. "Remember I told you that people are like books? There are good ones and bad ones, but they all teach a lesson. Don't ever let anyone convince you that one book is good or that another's bad. You read it and decide for yourself."

I helped Sister Nora place the tin boxes, the records, and the last layer of linen back inside the trunk. I thought about her childhood in Ireland. I wondered about other people I knew who, like Sister Nora and I, had come to America seeking a better life. How had Don Wong's life been before coming here? Or Herr Schmidt... what had he been through before coming to America?

Suddenly, a noise at the door made us both pause. Whoever stood behind it turned the knob slowly and didn't realize the door had been locked. The knob stopped turning, and the shadow at the bottom of the door stood still.

A jingling of keys broke the silence, and my eyes darted to Sister Nora, down to the open chest, and back to Sister Nora.

Her blue eyes never flinched. Instead, they locked on the door and narrowed.

thirty-three
POTFUL OF CHICKEN MOLE

I pointed to the chest and asked as quietly as I could, "Should we put this away?"

Sister Nora raised a hand, telling me to wait. She called out something in English toward the door.

The jingling stopped, but no one responded.

Sister Nora spoke again, this time in Spanish. "Can I help you?"

Noises of someone clearing their throat came through. A man's nervous voice followed in Spanish. "Sister Nora, I, uh...I didn't realize this was your room."

The voice came from Father Amaro, the new priest. According to Sister Nora, he'd been sent from Mexico City as a temporary substitute for the parish priest who'd recently fallen ill. Sister Nora wasn't too fond of Father Amaro because he often bragged about his Spanish ancestry and boasted about being born into one of Mexico's most prominent families.

Sister Nora scowled. "Is there something I can help you with?"

The shadow under the door remained still, and after a moment, Father Amaro cleared his throat once more. "I...I wanted to know what the plans are for tomorrow. What plans do you have for the guests' dinner?"

Sister Nora shut her eyes for a second and exhaled.

"Just a moment," she said and gently closed the lid to her chest. She signaled me to help push the trunk back under her bed.

I tilted my head, making sure the trunk had been pushed all the way in and was out of sight. Sister Nora dusted her hands before approaching the door as I remained on the floor.

"Good afternoon, Father Amaro." Sister Nora held the door open. "For dinner, Petra and I plan to cook tomato basil soup, roasted lamb chops, potatoes au gratin, and a vegetable medley."

The priest, with hands behind his back, didn't seem

to be listening to Sister Nora. Instead, he leaned in, stretched his neck, and scanned the room.

"Did you have a special request?" asked Sister Nora.

"What's for dessert?" asked the priest, not looking at Sister Nora.

Sister Nora gave me a glance. "I'm sending Petra to fetch some pan dulce—"

"No," Father Amaro chuckled. "Our guests deserve something more suitable to their taste." Father Amaro's gaze shifted to me. He gave a quick grimace before turning back to Sister Nora.

"What do you propose?" Sister Nora said.

"How about an almond torte, like the one you baked a few weeks back? Those generous contributions we received surely reflected your excellent cooking skills."

I knew what Father Amaro was trying to say. The guests who came to dinner at the church, the political exiles from Mexico, were wealthy, and it was important to keep them happy so they'd make donations.

Sister Nora showed no expression. "Almond torte it is."

"Wonderful," said the priest with a smile stamped across his face. He remained inside the room, shifting his eyes between Sister Nora and me, attempting to peek at the rest of the room.

"Anything else, Father Amaro?" asked Sister Nora.

"That's all." The young priest bowed his head and walked away.

The shuffling of his feet grew quieter the farther he got from us. Sister Nora left the door open and sat on her bed.

"Now that's a book I wish I could stop reading," she whispered.

"Is he a bad book?"

"No, he's not bad. Just annoying. All he ever does is talk about money or complain about people."

"Are we in trouble?"

Sister Nora shook her head. "The parish priest knows about the books. All he asked of me was discretion."

"Why? Does the church not like the books?"

"The church forbids certain books because it believes they will alter people's faith."

I thought back to all the things Sister Nora had taught me from the books. My faith didn't feel altered. If anything, it felt stronger. Only my mind had changed. New ideas and visions buzzed in and out of my mind, and I couldn't wait to share it all with Abuelita, Camila, Amelia, and even Nina and Luisito. Maybe Abuelita's mind would change too and she'd be less afraid of new moons and smoking stars.

That evening, as I helped Abuelita and Camila with dinner, I told them all I'd learned about planets, comets, and stars. I told them about *la Vía Láctea*, the Milky Way, and how it got its name.

Amelia sat on a chair with Luisito on her lap. Nina, sitting across from them, fed Luisito spoonfuls of *arroz con leche* while sneaking one for herself every now and then. I'd made Amelia promise me not to ask anything until I was done talking, but her feet twitched and jittered in anticipation. As I continued to talk, Camila gasped and gave me wide-eyed glances as if I were sharing the juiciest gossip ever. Abuelita, on the other hand, shook her head and crossed herself constantly as if I were sharing nothing but bad news.

"I never knew the Earth spun," said Camila. "No wonder I feel so dizzy sometimes."

In my excitement, I continued to talk and then said something I probably should've saved for later. I talked about the man named Darwin, and when I tried to explain evolution, Abuelita almost dropped the big pot of chicken mole.

"Who in God's name is putting those ridiculous ideas in your head?" said Abuelita.

"They're not ridiculous ideas, Abuelita," I said. "It's all real. It's in the books."

"Señora," Camila turned to Abuelita, "Petra's brain is growing. That's a good thing."

Abuelita's face grew red. "*Esas cosas son del diablo.* Those are works of the devil." She immediately crossed herself three times and whispered a prayer because the word *devil* had escaped her lips.

"What if Sister Nora found out about the things you're saying?" Abuelita said. "About your talk of monkeys and nonsense? Imagine how upset she'd be."

I remained quiet. My plan had backfired. Abuelita didn't become less fearful. Instead, she was upset and believed my mind was full of evil inklings.

Night fell over our quiet shack, and after spreading my blankets on the floor, I made my way to the bed to cover a sleeping Luisito. I also tucked Amelia under the covers. She was still awake.

"Petra," Amelia said. "Could you tell me more about what you learned from the books?"

I paused. Abuelita and Camila's voices sounded relaxed as they chatted outside with one of the neighbors.

"You can't tell Abuelita," I said.

"I won't. I promise."

I knelt beside the bed. "We live in this big, beautiful planet called *Tierra*. It's like a giant ball that—"

"Wait." Amelia propped herself up on her elbows. "I forgot to tell you. Don Wong only has three slates left. Can we buy one soon before he runs out?"

"Not now," I said. "We need to save money again."

"Are you afraid Sister Nora might fire you like the chili queen?"

"No, Sister Nora is different. We just need to save money to go find Papa."

"But you need a slate to learn to read and write— that's your dream."

"Sister Nora's already teaching me a little."

Amelia sighed and lay back down. "Maybe one day I can buy it for you."

"One day," I said and gently pinched her cheek.

Amelia scooted toward Luisito, making room for me to lie next to her. I began telling her about the Earth, the sun, and the moon. I would start slow, but eventually, I wanted to teach her and Luisito everything I knew. With all my heart, I believed every time we learned something new, we were one step closer to clearing our lives of ghosts, superstitions, and fears.

thirty-four

A SCENT OF JASMINE

When I arrived at the church the next morning, Sister Nora, sipping on a hot lemon tea in the courtyard, told me about the two special guests who'd be visiting and staying in the church quarters.

"It appears every hotel room in San Antonio has been booked," Sister Nora said.

"How old are the girls?" I asked. If they were my age, we'd have more in common than just escaping the revolution.

"I didn't ask," Sister Nora said. "All I know is that one of the girls is a Bentacur—one of the wealthiest families in Mexico."

With those words, I realized I probably wouldn't have much in common with them.

"Today I need you to scrub the chapel floors then sweep the front of the church," Sister Nora said. "Once you get done with that, come in and help me prepare the lunch for the two guests. Any questions?"

"No, ma'am," I said.

"Before you go do your chores," Sister Nora said, "let's do our morning search."

Two weeks before, after making sure I knew how to write my first name, Sister Nora had taught me to write my last name, Luna, and my father's first name, Alonso. Every morning since then, before handing the Spanish newspaper to Father Amaro, Sister Nora and I would go over the section that listed the names of refugees seeking loved ones. Each message appeared in a little box. The message Sister Nora and I paid to have listed in the paper was always near the top. After making sure it was there, I would quickly scan through the other messages to see if I recognized my name or my father's.

So far, it hadn't happened, and this morning was no exception.

It was almost ten o'clock when I started sweeping the front of the church. I noticed my shoes had gotten muddy from the courtyard, so I stopped to take them off, along with my stockings, to dry off. I'd resumed sweeping when an automobile pulled in front of the church.

A man in a dark suit stepped out and walked around to open the automobile's back door. He helped a young lady wearing a long, white silk dress step out. She seemed to be about seventeen, and her gloved hand went up to block the sunlight from her eyes as she took in the church bell towers. Her pose and her long neck were as elegant as a swan's, and the soft waves of her auburn hair gently framed her face.

Another young lady stepped out of the automobile. She too wore silk, but her pose was less graceful, and her voice sounded like a duck's dull quack.

She called out to the auburn-haired girl. "Aren't you forgetting something, Victoria?"

Victoria—her name was as beautiful as she was. The duck-voiced girl handed Victoria a folded hand fan, which Victoria immediately spanned open and began to fan herself with.

It dawned on me that these were the two girls Sister Nora said would stay in the church's quarters.

The man in the dark suit set two suitcases on the

sidewalk and tipped his hat at them before returning to his automobile and driving away.

The young lady with the quack voice glanced over at me and winced when she saw my bare feet. She turned away. "Grab my luggage and take it in," she said.

I glanced at my shoes sitting by the door. The mud on them still looked fresh, and I didn't want to dirty the floor I had scrubbed earlier.

"Did you not hear me?" she said, placing a hand on her hip. "Grab my belongings and take them inside." Her glare and her tone stung. It took me back to a time and place in Mexico where people like her scolded people like me.

She turned to Victoria. "Is this india deaf, or is she just a simpleton?"

Vitoria chuckled, fanning herself and looking at the buildings around us. "Ay, Elena, the suitcases are small. We can carry them ourselves."

"That's not the point," said Elena. "It's her job to—"

Victoria raised her hand to Elena as if motioning to her to be quiet. She then turned to me, and in a swift motion, she folded her fan and pointed it to herself. "I'm Victoria Bentacur de los Santos." She then pointed

THE OTHER SIDE OF THE RIVER

to the other young woman. "And this is my friend, Elena Urquiza Echeverri."

Their names sounded elegant, and though I was sure they were Spanish, they were names I'd never heard before.

"Y tú?" said Victoria. "Cómo te llamas?" Her deep-green eyes beamed, and her smile calmed my anger.

"Petra," I said. "Me llamo Petra Luna."

Elena snickered, bringing her gloved hand to her mouth.

"What?" said Victoria. "There's nothing wrong with a simple name. I find Luna to be a very poetic name."

I felt myself blush.

"Let's get something straight, Petra," Elena said, "if you address me, it's Niña Elena to you. That's how our servants in Mexico addressed me before this stupid revolution took everything away."

I looked at Elena's jeweled necklace that glimmered under the sun, her silks, and her full belly and round cheeks, and wondered what was the "everything" the revolution had taken away.

Victoria gave a slight eye roll. "Elena, will you let it go? We're not in Mexico nor in Paris. We're in America. Get used it."

"I've never been to Paris," Elena said, placing her gloves in a small purse covered in shiny beads, "but you're right. This definitely isn't Mexico." With a huff, she grabbed her suitcase and walked into the church.

Victoria chuckled as her gaze followed Elena into the church. "She hates it here."

I was surprised she was talking to me. Part of me wanted to ask why Elena hated being here. What had Elena lost in the revolution? Had Victoria also lost everything? But I decided to keep the questions to myself.

"I best catch up with her." Victoria grabbed her suitcase. "I'll see you around."

I nodded and watched Victoria walk up the stairs and into the church, leaving a scent of jasmine behind. I inhaled the flowery scent, and for the first time in my life, my insides didn't twist at the smell of the fancy perfume.

Maybe the revolution in Mexico was slowly changing things. Perhaps Victoria's mind had changed. She didn't seem to view me the same way Elena did.

In the afternoon, while cleaning up after lunch, I told Sister Nora about Elena, about the way she'd spoken to me, and about how she'd asked me to call her Niña Elena, like her servants in Mexico.

"Shenanigans," Sister Nora said.

I didn't know what the word meant, but from the way Sister Nora's face grew red as she said it, I guessed it was probably a swear word.

thirty-five

TWO PERFECT SNOWFLAKES

It took me more than twenty tries to get the word *shenanigans* to roll smoothly off my tongue.

"It means mischief or trickery," Sister Nora said. Her face grew redder the more she spoke. "But to me it also means dishonest or unscrupulous behavior. When that girl asked you to address her as *niña*, she's either ignorant or deceitful. For starters, you're my employee, not hers. And second, you're not a servant."

Then it dawned on me. We too had a Spanish word for shenanigans. It was *chanchullos*.

Sister Nora's knife fell on the vegetables a lot harder than usual.

"When I was in Mexico," she said, "it upset me to see how much one country could mistreat its own people.

I can't blame people for rising up, for wanting a better life."

She took a deep breath to calm herself. Then she looked at me. "I've never told you about how Róisín and I came to America from Ireland, have I?"

I shook my head. I wanted to hear more about Róisín, and maybe talking about her would make Sister Nora feel better.

She placed a yellow squash on the board. "My grandmother, bless her soul, got passes for Róisín and me to sail to America."

"Your grandmother didn't sail with you?" I asked.

"No, she was only able to secure two passes."

I thought about the day I had crossed the bridge to America and how Amelia and Luisito and I had become separated from Abuelita. I could still see the anguish on Abuelita's face as she pushed us to cross the bridge alone. I couldn't imagine our lives without her.

"Was Róisín upset?" I asked.

Sister Nora nodded, slicing the squash. "The old woman who was to look out for us died during the voyage. Probably starved to death. There's a reason those ships were called coffin ships. Food was scarce.

Filth was everywhere. The entire ship smelled of waste and death. By the time we reached America, Róisín was sick too."

"But she got better, right?"

Sister Nora sighed. "We arrived in a city called Boston and had no idea where to go. We met a boy who spoke Gaelic. He was dressed better than us, he wore shoes, and he offered Róisín work and shelter. We thought we'd struck gold. He asked for a deposit for our room, and after Róisín gave him all the coins we had, the boy disappeared. We were left with nothing, and Róisín was crushed."

I thought about times I had felt so crushed and help-less too. Like when I had to beg in front of a church to save Luisito's life.

"Did Róisín look for work or beg for alms?" I asked.

"She could barely walk, and when we asked strangers for work or help, they'd say 'I don't hire Irish.' The few people who looked at us shot us glares that were as cold as the icy puddles our bare feet walked through."

"I don't understand," I said, my voice breaking. "Were these people whiter than you?"

Sister Nora laughed a little. "It's not about color. When people see others in inferior positions—barefoot, wearing ragged clothes, or uneducated—they assume it's because they're lazy or unintelligent or are content being poor."

"But Róisín got better, right?" I asked again.

"I wish I could say she had," Sister Nora said. "Two days after our arrival, Róisín was already coughing up blood. At night, we snuggled against the warm vent of a building and wrapped ourselves in newspapers. I pressed my ear against Róisín's chest and swore I heard a small wolf growling inside her. The next morning when I opened my eyes, I saw a giant snowflake fall gently over Róisín's chest. I sat up, put my hand out, and two snowflakes fell into my hand."

Sister Nora looked at her palm and used her fingers to trace the snowflakes she'd seen.

"They were perfect. Umblemished. I turned to Róisín and saw how the scattered snowflakes stood out against her long, red hair, and how still she was. I tried to wake her so she could see the perfect snowflakes, but I couldn't. She never opened her eyes again."

"That's terrible," I said, wiping my eyes and nose and imagining the helplessness Róisín must have felt on her last night.

"Róisín made sure I was taken care of until her last breath," Sister Nora said. "Thanks to her I've had a wonderful life. I wound up in an orphanage, and there were some bitter moments, but life has also blessed me with many breathtaking experiences."

Sister Nora turned to me. "That's why I enjoy talking to you so much, Petra. I feel like I'm talking to Róisín all over again."

thirty-six
TREETOPS & SERENADES

Two days later, Sister Nora rushed into the chapel where I was dusting. "I have news for you," she said with a bright smile across her face.

I dropped the feather duster and hopped off the step stool. "Is it Papa? Do you have news about him?"

Sister Nora gave me a wry expression. "No, I'm sorry. It's about a new school being opened near the Wesley House. Have you heard?"

I shook my head. I'd hoped for news about Papa, but I was eager to hear about the new school.

"It'll have a nursery for children like Luisito," Sister Nora said, "a kindergarten for kids like Amelia, and day and night classes for children like you."

I blinked my eyes. "That means Amelia and

Luisito can start going to school," I said. "And me too."

"Yes," Sister Nora said, "And yesterday, I spoke to the school's director, Mr. Knox, and he told me about a position he's trying to fill. I told him you'd be the perfect person for it."

I cringed.

"What's the matter, child? I thought you'd be ecstatic."

"I like working for you," I said. "I thought you liked me too."

"Of course, I like you. Just because you don't work here doesn't mean we can't stay in touch. You're like family to me."

I nodded. "But if I'm going to clean the school, I'd rather clean the church, run errands, and do the shopping with you."

"The work has nothing to do with cleaning or running errands," Sister Nora said. "The school needs a translator. They need someone who can help them communicate with all the refugee children attending the school."

"But I...I can't..." I didn't know how to tell Sister Nora

that I wanted the work, but deep down inside, I believed it was something I couldn't do. I didn't want to disappoint her. "It's just my English isn't—"

"Petra, I've never seen anyone learn English as fast as you. Besides, the school won't open until March. That gives you about four months to improve your English."

My stomach knotted. "Will the pay be the same as here?"

"I didn't ask, but I bet it's the same or more. And by March, you'll be able to teach children their letters too."

Me, a teacher? The thought filled my lungs with so much air, I felt I could fly.

On my way home, I stopped to sit on the edge of a fountain in the middle of Military Plaza, and thought about what Sister Nora had told me.

Hundreds of grackles dominated the sky and treetops in the plaza. Their black feathers glistened in the soft light of the setting sun. They flew from treetop to treetop as if deciding which one was best to settle in for the night. Their harsh and usually annoying song blended gently with the crisp autumn breeze, and to me it sounded like a serenade.

At dinner, I told Abuelita and Camila about the new school near the Wesley House.

Amelia's mouth dropped open. "I'm going to school?"

"You are," I said. A spark of triumph lit inside me. I prayed this plan worked out.

"If the school you're talking about is just up the street," Camila said, "Amelia and Nina could walk there together." She rubbed Nina's head, and Nina gave her usual quiet smile.

"And both girls can take Luisito," Abuelita said.

I took in everyone's excitement. "And if I get a job there, I can take them all."

"A job there?" Abuelita asked. "How will you get a job there?"

"Sister Nora said the school director is hiring a person to help people who just came from Mexico talk to people who only speak English."

"Bah! You don't even speak English." Abuelita said.

"I speak a little English," I said.

"No," said Camila. "You speak more than a little. I've heard you before, at the Wesley House."

I turned to Abuelita. "Sister Nora said that, with time, I could probably start teaching children their letters and numbers in English too."

Amelia gasped. "You're going to be a teacher? Maybe you can be my teacher. And Nina's too." Her smile turned to worry. "You need to get that slate from Don Wong's now so you can start practicing being a teacher. But you better hurry because he only has one left."

Abuelita gave a look of annoyance. "M'ija, do you really need a new job? You're doing so well at the church."

"Ay, Señora," said Camila. "The job will be good for Petra. This can help her find work later at a hospital or an office."

Abuelita raised her eyebrows. "A hospital? An office?" She flapped her hands in front of her as if dismissing the whole thing. "That kind of work is for gringos. We Mexicans were made for labor. God blessed us with strong hands and strong bodies to withstand labor under any condition."

Camila scratched the back of her head but kept quiet.

"Get those crazy ideas out of your head," said Abuelita. "You have a great job already, and you might lose it if you start looking into foolish things like working for some school director."

Abuelita stood from the table, and before she left the room, she turned to me. "*Acuérdate*, remember, you're a Mexican, and a Mexican girl at that. Just because you wear pretty shoes and nice clothes now doesn't mean you belong with the gringos. Their world is different, and we'll never be part of it."

Camila made sure Abuelita was gone before she took a deep breath and turned to me with a soft smile.

"Why is she like that?" I asked. "It's like she hates that I'm getting a better job."

"You have to understand her," Camila said. "Your grandmother grew up in a different time when gringos were wealthy mine owners, untouchable. But you, Petra, you work with them. You do business with them. Things are different for you."

"You want me to tell Don Wong to save the slate for you?" asked Amelia. "I won't tell Abuelita about it."

I shook my head, looking in the direction my grandmother had taken. "No. I don't know. Let's just wait."

As I lay down to sleep, I thought back to the plaza, to the grackles that flew from tree to tree. I too had flown from chopping wood in Mexico, to taking orders from a chili queen, to helping and learning from an Irish nun. I was certain I was about to fly onto another treetop and couldn't wait to do it.

thirty-seven

THE BLUE DANUBE

Throughout the next day, as we did the shopping and cooking, Sister Nora gave me glances and secretive smiles, like she wanted to tell me something but couldn't. I knew it wasn't about the newspaper and our search for Papa because we'd already read it that morning. But once we'd served lunch to Victoria, Elena, and Father Amaro and were cleaning up, Sister Nora spoke.

"I have something to show you," she said.

"A new book?" I said, hoping there'd been a new addition to her trunk.

"No, but just as good. Come, let me show you."

Sister Nora took my hand and led me to the choir room, the same room where I'd lost my baby diamond. She walked to the tall windows and pulled open the giant, heavy drapes, and the room filled with sunshine.

"A friend loaned this to me last night," Sister Nora said, motioning to a wooden box with a large tin horn attached to it. A small metal plate on the corner of the box had the image of the dog I'd seen on Sister Nora's records.

I gasped. "It's a talking machine. Can you make music come out of it?"

"I need to wind it first." Sister Nora turned a small side handle, giving it several spins, before she took a record out of its envelope.

"Let's see if you recognize this." She placed the record on the machine and tapped on a tiny lever that caused the disc to spin. Slowly, she placed the needle on the record and turned to me. A warm, raspy sound came out of the tin horn. The sound of bells followed, and when the music started, my heart leaped.

"It's the song from that night," I said. "The one the choirboys were singing."

"Yes," said Sister Nora, "you've got a great ear."

Flashbacks of that night, of when I'd lost my black rock, came to me, with the same goose bumps.

Once the song was over, Sister Nora grabbed another record and switched it.

"Have you ever waltzed before?"

I shook my head repeatedly. "That's only for fancy people."

Sister Nora wrinkled her brow, pulling back her chin. "Music and dance aren't prejudiced. You can sing and dance to whatever music your heart desires."

Sister Nora set the needle down on the record and extended her arms to me. "Come."

The soft music started slow, and I giggled as Sister Nora bowed in front of me and asked me to return the formal greeting. She told me to grab the side of my skirt, bend my knees, and bow my head slightly. Afterward, she grabbed my left hand and placed it over her right shoulder, and when she grabbed my right hand, she said, "Let this one rest over my hand."

"What song is this?" I asked.

"'*En el Bello Danubio Azul*,'" she said.

I had no idea what a Danube was. Perhaps it was a flowery meadow with an open blue sky, or a tall, tall castle overlooking a bright blue sea. But as the music played, I soared over every place I imagined.

Sister Nora gently pressed her palm against my back. "Keep your back straight and your elbows almost at shoulder height," she said. "Chin up. Shoulders back."

I nodded and followed Sister Nora's lead. We shuffled our feet, taking a sidestep with one foot and closing in with the other, over and over again. We swayed from side to side, and I imagined us like two strong ships sailing over big ocean waves. We moved our feet along a small imaginary square on the floor, and I couldn't help but laugh every time I stepped on Sister Nora's shoes or tripped over my own feet.

I snorted. "I can't keep up with you."

"This is no laughing matter," said Sister Nora. "You never know who will ask you to waltz."

At one point, when the music's pace increased, I think Sister Nora forgot about the imaginary square. We spun and twirled around the floor like planets in a musical solar system. A cross, attached to Sister Nora's rosary, hung from the waist of her robe and swayed along with us.

I could tell the waltz was about to end because the music grew louder and more powerful. Sister Nora and

I spun faster, and everything around me became a blur except for the music and her smile. Sister Nora loved to dance as much as she loved books.

The music stopped, and even though we had stopped moving, everything around us still whirled. I felt dizzy, and I didn't know if it was from spinning or from the excitement of having learned to waltz.

A voice, as warm and as raspy as the sounds of the record, shouted, "Bravo! Bravo!" It was Victoria, clapping at us. Elena, standing farther behind, also clapped but not as enthusiastically.

"I had no idea nuns could waltz," Victoria said. Her bright green eyes grew in admiration of Sister Nora.

"Sister Nora is not like other nuns," I said sheepishly.

"I see that," Victoria said, glancing back at Elena, who fanned herself. Elena's face told everyone she'd rather be elsewhere.

"Care to join us for a dance?" Sister Nora placed a different record on the machine.

"Another waltz?" Victoria asked.

"No," Sister Nora said. "This one is Gaelic music." She turned to me. "This is the Irish music I grew up with."

Sister Nora placed the needle down, and through the tinhorn came low, steady drumbeats mixed with another instrument. Sister Nora clapped to the beat. I followed with steady claps too, turning to Victoria. She too began clapping. Different instruments joined the song, and what happened next astounded me.

Sister Nora lifted her robe just below the knee and kicked off her shoes, showing us all her black stockings. She held her robe up and kicked and stomped like no other person, or nun, I'd ever seen before.

"Join me," Sister Nora shouted over the fast-paced music.

I lifted my skirt and mimicked Sister Nora's feet as they kicked to the rhythm. She signaled Victoria and Elena to join us. Victoria hesitated and turned to Elena, who shrugged and continued to fan her long, bored face.

The music had paused, except for the beating of the drums, which played faster.

"Some things are better when you're barefoot," said Sister Nora, fumbling to remove her stockings. She motioned her chin toward our feet "Take them off."

Giggling at each other, Victoria and I removed our shoes and stockings. Soon, all three of us held our dresses up and danced to the swift fiddle and drums with nothing to hamper our happy feet. I imitated Sister Nora's joyful shouts, and when she extended her arms to me, I took them.

There was no straightening of the back in this dance, and it reminded me a lot of the dancing in Mexico but with a whole lot more hopping. Victoria and I laughed over and over at the silly faces Sister Nora made, not knowing if they were part of the dance.

"I feel Irish," I told Sister Nora as we spun with our hands clasped together. "I even feel proud listening to this music, and I'm Mexican."

Sister Nora laughed and winked an eye. "You're living the music."

We both locked our arms at the elbow and spun around, switching arms from time to time. Victoria, swaying her body side to side, watched us and clapped to the music.

As the song neared its end, all three of us held hands and formed a small circle. We continued to hop to the music and brought ourselves together repeatedly by raising our hands to the center of the circle and bringing them back down.

I felt as if I were in another world, a happy one where three people from completely different places came together. Never in my wildest dreams did I ever see myself dancing with a nun, much less with a fancy lady from Mexico. Things were clearly different in America.

thirty-eight
THREE RAVENS

Three days later, I awoke to the low rumble of thunder as the soft rain pelted our tin roof. On the floor, next to me, lay Abuelita's folded blankets. The yellow glow of the kitchen light seeped through the fabric hanging across the doorway.

"What time is it?" I said, stepping into the kitchen.

"Too early," Abuelita said. "I forgot to put the corn husks to soak last night."

I glanced at Camila's clock. It was a little past six.

"Go back to bed, m'ija. I'll wake you in an hour."

I shook my head, yawning. "I got paid yesterday. I need to give you the money for this week's shopping."

I walked to the row of potted herbs Abuelita kept near the stove. I reached for the overgrown oregano plant and lifted it by the pot, which sat inside a big, rusty can. At the bottom of the old can lay a small tin box where we stored all our money.

I pulled the small box out and accidentally knocked the old can down. It bounced and rattled inside an empty wooden crate on the floor.

"Shhh," Abuelita said. "Don't wake the children."

"Why is the crate empty? Has Amelia not gone out to gather pecans?"

"Too much rain," said Abuelita. "She wanted to go to the creek yesterday, but I didn't want her to catch a cold. She said she wants to get us Christmas gifts."

I set aside money for Abuelita to buy the groceries and some for the rent. I put all the coins and bills together to count our savings.

"Five dollars and twenty cents," I said.

Abuelita nodded and gave a gesture of approval.

"Has it been raining all night?" I asked.

"It hasn't stopped since last night," Abuelita said, cleaning the insides of the dried chili pods and inspecting them for any seeds she may have missed.

I put the remaining money back in the tin box and placed it back under the oregano plant. I got ready for work, careful not to wake Amelia or Luisito, who were cuddled with each other like puppies.

The rain had stopped by the time I'd reached the church, but a thick blanket of clouds threatened us with more showers. I sat in the kitchen looking over the newspaper, hoping as always to find Papa's name. Ever since I'd arrived this morning, Sister Nora had been rushing around the kitchen. She swiftly grabbed things from the pantry, pots from the cabinet, and gathered everything around the table. Halfway through searching for Papa's name on the paper, I looked up at Sister Nora. "Has this ever worked? Have people actually found family this way?"

Sister Nora mumbled to herself as she searched through a drawer.

"You seem rushed," I said. "Are you nervous about cooking today's big dinner?"

Sister Nora stopped and turned to me. "No—I'm sorry—I'm getting things prepared before I leave."

"Before you leave?" I put the newspaper down on the table. For a moment I feared Father Amaro had probably found her hidden books and was sending her away. "Are you in trouble? Where are you going?"

"No." Sister Nora gave a me a tender smile. "I'm not in trouble. I have to head north, to a small town called Leon Springs, only for a couple of days." Sister Nora took a sip of her steaming cup. "A lady there needs me to help her deliver her baby."

"Why didn't you tell me earlier? And why do you have to go? Are there no midwives there?"

"I think it's best that I go. Mrs. Shultz trusts me and wants me there. When she lived in San Antonio, I helped her through two complicated births. She sent for me early this morning."

I looked outside. The sky seemed darker and a lot more eerie. Today was a big day. Father Amaro was hosting an important dinner for Mr. Knox.

"What about tonight's dinner?" I said, looking at the many spices, measuring cups and spoons set on the table. "I can't do it all by myself. And besides, you said you'd introduce me to Mr. Knox."

"You'll be fine, child," said Sister Nora, "I spoke to Father Amaro and told him you're capable of running things here on your own. Don't worry about Mr. Knox. I'll introduce you two when I get back." Sister Nora stopped herself from walking back into the pantry.

"And before I forget…" She reached into her pocket and pulled out a white envelope. "Should anything happen to me, here's—"

"Why would anything happen to you?" I suddenly felt ill.

"No, it's just…" Sister Nora exhaled, setting the envelope on the table. "I have this ill feeling. This morning I saw three ravens in the courtyard, and I've felt uneasy ever since. Perhaps it's a sign that I need to be with Mrs. Shultz." Sister Nora hurried into the pantry and returned to the table with more items. "I'm sure it's nothing—"

"Of course, it's nothing," I said. I didn't understand how someone who had taught me about spinning planets and the origins of life believed three ravens brought bad luck. "Why would you let three birds push you to take a trip?"

"It's not about the birds," Sister Nora said. "Or maybe it is, just a little, but something tells me I need to make that trip."

I felt dozens of grasshoppers jumping inside me. "What's in the envelope?"

Sister Nora fumbled through a recipe book. "A

character letter for you. It's a written testimonial of your character. I want you to save the letter and give it to Mr. Knox when he interviews you. Also, next week, don't forget to register yourself and your siblings for school."

My chest felt heavy, talking about things I had to do in the future, and the thought of Sister Nora not being with me, made me queasy.

"I hate to leave this way," Sister Nora said, "But I assure you it's going to be fine."

Sister Nora gave me instructions on what I needed to shop for, prepare, and cook to create the perfect dinner for Father Amaro's guests. This would be an important dinner because they'd discuss ways to fund Mr. Knox's new school. Maybe, if I felt confident enough, I'd introduce myself to Mr. Knox. But before doing that, I'd have to impress him with a special dinner.

Sister Nora left for the train station, and I did the morning shopping alone under a drizzling sky. When I arrived at the church, I struggled to carry the wet and slippery baskets full of groceries into the church. My arms felt as if they'd break in half as I lifted the baskets and set them gently on the kitchen table. As I rubbed the soreness in my arms, I caught sight of the folded newspaper. I hadn't finished reading all the names on the page.

I spread the newspaper over the kitchen table and began emptying the baskets as I read each block aloud to myself. Suddenly, I saw a name that made me drop the onions I held in my hands.

With my heart thumping in my ears, I grabbed the newspaper and brought it closer to me. My hands couldn't stop shaking, and my eyes strained to focus on the letters, but there it was, Papa's name: *Alonso Luna.*

My eyes skimmed through the rest of the message. Raindrops had smudged part of it, but what I could read was that Alonso wanted to meet his daughter at three o'clock on Tuesday afternoon at the newspaper office. I dashed to the calendar that hung near the pantry door to assure myself today was the right day, and it was. Today was Tuesday, the day I was to reunite with Papa.

thirty-nine
ENTWINED

I had two important things to accomplish today: reunite with Papa and impress Mr. Knox with the best meal he'd ever had. I only had a few hours to pull both off.

With almost a constant eye on the clock, I quickly prepared everything I needed to cook for the big dinner. I cleaned up after myself as fast as I could. I wanted to have enough time to rush home and take Abuelita and Amelia with me to the newspaper office to meet Papa. I ran out of the church toward the streetcar stop, but my excitement and urge to share the greatest news of my life—of having Papa back in our lives—made me run all the way home.

Out of breath, I still managed to shout out Abuelita's

and Amelia's names as I reached the porch of our shack. "I've got incredible news!" I called out as I walked through the door. But inside, it was silent.

Abuelita's apron hung from the back of a chair. Her sweater and Amelia's yellow coat were missing from the wall's hooks. They'd probably gone to the Wesley House, or Don Wong's store, or somewhere else.

I looked at Camila's clock. Three o'clock was less than an hour away. If I waited too long here, I'd run the risk of missing Papa. What if I had trouble finding the newspaper office? What if Papa only had a few minutes to spare? What if he was only passing through and today was his only time in San Antonio? I couldn't take that chance.

I stepped out onto the porch and looked both ways down the alley of the wasp's nest. The rain had started again, and there were no signs of Abuelita or Amelia coming home. I imagined myself coming back at dusk and walking through the door arm in arm with Papa. The thought alone was thrilling enough to make me change my mind about taking Abuelita and Amelia with me.

I ran back to the streetcar stop and found it full

of people. Men glanced at their watches and women looked down Flores Street for a view of the streetcar. I learned everyone had been waiting for at least thirty minutes. I waited for another five minutes before I decided to run to the newspaper office instead. It was north of downtown, and I still had a chance to get there before three o'clock.

I bolted through muddy alleyways and neighborhood backstreets. My lungs burned, and I gripped my black rock, envisioning myself calling out Papa's name and him running to me. I pictured all of us—Papa, Abuelita, Pablo, Sister Nora, Camila, myself, and all the kids—sitting around a large table. In front of us, there'd be plates topped with tamales, chiles rellenos, *frijoles rancheros*, chicharrones, and plenty of pan pobre for all of us. And just like the fancy people, we'd raise our cups of champurrado and toast to Papa's return.

I stopped at the corner where the newspaper office stood. The clock on the street corner signaled I had made it with seconds to spare. I swiftly combed my damp hair with my fingers, straightened my skirt, and stomped my feet to make sure my boots weren't too muddy. I flattened the ends of my purple scarf, raised my chin high, and walked over to meet Papa.

I turned the corner and saw a man and a woman halfway down the block. From a distance, I could see the woman wearing nice clothes, but unlike her, the man wore ragged clothes: white pants, white shirt, and sandals. He held a straw hat in front of him as he spoke to the woman. I couldn't see his face, but he seemed to be the right height. I hadn't remembered Papa's shoulders being that broad, but maybe they were. I increased my pace. My heart, my breathing, my blinking—everything ran wild inside me.

I got closer and managed to say, "Papa?"

The man swung his head in my direction and smiled. It wasn't Papa. My eyes turned to the building. Perhaps Papa was inside, or maybe he was running late.

When I turned back to the man, he was looking at me with happy, eager eyes. I swallowed. "*Busco a* Alonso Luna," I said, hoping he'd point to Papa's whereabouts. I squeezed my black rock hard inside my fist.

"Alonso Luna?" said the man, taking a step closer to me.

"Yes," I said.

The man's smile faded. He glanced at his huaraches, his sandals, took a deep breath, and then turned back to me. "My name is Alfonso Luna. Not Alonso."

"But I read the paper myself," I said. "It was my Papa's name I read—Alonso Luna."

The man pulled the folded paper out of his pocket and pointed to his name. He was right. It did say Alfonso. I looked down, convinced I'd see my heart shattered on the ground. "I'm sorry," I said. It hurt to breathe.

"No worries, muchacha," he said with damp eyes. "We'll both keep looking, and one day, we'll find our loved ones."

He excused himself, put his hat on, and walked away with hands in his pockets and eyes looking down. The woman patted my shoulder before returning to the building, and I was left alone on the sidewalk, entwined with an immense pain that kept my feet locked in place.

forty

BROKEN EGGSHELLS

Darkness took over the day, and a light drizzle fell over the city. I walked back to the church. Its kitchen seemed cold without Sister Nora. I had a sick feeling in the pit of my stomach, but I told myself it'd be gone if I focused on my work.

I opened Sister Nora's cookbook to the bookmark she'd set in place. My eyes gazed at the recipe. I recognized words like *salt*, *sugar*, and *vinegar*, *cup*, *teaspoon*, and *pinch*. How could I have misread Papa's name? Perhaps Sister Nora was wrong about me becoming a teacher. Perhaps I shouldn't introduce myself to Mr. Knox tonight after all because cooking a great feast didn't matter when I didn't know how to read.

I took a basket of eggs and sat them next to a bowl.

As I cracked each one, the crumbling sound of thunder echoed in the quiet kitchen. I thought about the strength of the eggshell, of how it was strong enough to hold life, but a single tap in the right place broke the whole thing apart. Were people the same? Did I have a point that would break me completely apart?

As I finished preparing the dinner, the guests began to arrive. I recognized Victoria's voice right away. I was surprised to hear how well Mr. Knox spoke Spanish.

An hour passed, and somehow, I had managed to cook the main course, side dishes and serve them all. Once I had cleaned the kitchen and served the coffee and dessert, I stood quietly behind the thin curtain that opened to the dining room, hoping to overhear their plans for the new school. The darkness of the hallway hid me well, and I could see everyone except for Victoria, Father Amaro, and Mr. Knox.

"We find America to be...different," said Elena's mother. "We miss Mexico City very much."

"I like it here," said Victoria. "It's no Paris or Mexico City, but it'll do for now."

"That's true," Elena's mother said. "I'd forgotten you

lived in Paris. We had plans to travel there, but with this obnoxious revolution, it'll have to wait."

"Have you been to Paris, Mr. Knox?" Victoria asked.

"I have," Mr. Knox said.

"I'm impressed, Señor Knox" Elena's mother said.

"But not the one in France," Mr. Knox said. "I've been to the one here in Texas. Paris, Texas."

Elena's mother raised an eyebrow and went back to eating her dessert.

"You all would love it," said Victoria. "It's almost like Mexico City, except their buildings are grander and more gorgeous, and their parks are more beautiful than Chapultepec."

"What about the shopping?" Elena's mother asked.

"It's glorious," Victoria said. "But the best part about Paris is its refined people. Everyone is dressed impeccably. Not like in Mexico City, where you constantly come across *chusma*."

My heart was suddenly on fire, but maybe I'd misunderstood Victoria. Perhaps when she mentioned the riffraff, she referred to something else.

"We attended one of President Díaz's parades in 1910," Elena's mother continued, "as we celebrated his reelection, he made sure none of those pitiful people spoiled the grand event. Can you imagine the embarrassment if foreign dignitaries saw those people wearing their filthy, ragged clothes and begging for alms?"

It was my people Elena's mother spoke of, but I was sure Victoria didn't agree with her.

"Ever since our arrival"—Victoria had lowered her voice—"I avoid going anywhere near the train depot. Have you noticed how those people have settled in that part of the city?"

Father Amaro spoke up. "Some people call it Los Corrales because it looks like a *chiquero*, a pig's pen."

Laughter broke out, and I wondered if Victoria and Mr. Knox had laughed too.

"Mr. Knox," said Victoria's father. "Your intent to open your school in that neighborhood concerns us. Many of our friends have small children and would benefit from the school in a different location."

Mr. Knox didn't respond.

"Señor Bentacur may have a point," Father Amaro said. "Your school could make the transition of their children into American life easier."

Elena's mother cleared her throat. "Perhaps a nice

contribution would allow you to open the school in a nice part of the city, maybe purchase a new building."

"Gracias," Mr. Knox said. "Your contribution would indeed help us build a school."

I stood there not believing what I heard—Victoria and her family, along with Father Amaro, trying to take away our only chance to learn and improve our lives.

"Mr. Knox," Victoria said, "You must understand, these people are not the same as us."

Victoria's words were like a kick in the gut. Hadn't she seen me as a friend? Hadn't she asked my name, smiled at me, talked to me, and even danced with me?

Vitoria's mother interrupted. "What my darling daughter means is that impoverished children have no time for school. They're busy working, attending to chores, so it's useless to force these children to go to school."

"They're not like us," Victoria said. "The way they live, eat—it's appalling. Two days ago, the smell of corn bread lingered around here, and it was revolting."

"That was Petra," Father Amaro said. "She and Sister Nora are always cooking it."

"Corn is for pigs, for donkeys," Victoria's mother said. "It's a deplorable grain."

"That's interesting," Mr. Knox said. "I eat corn bread almost every day."

"Eating corn bread is not a horrible thing," Elena's mother said. "What's truly revolting are *nodrizas* who are indias. When I found out Elena's former fiancé had been nursed as an infant by one of his family's servant girls—an india—ay, Dios." Elena's mother brought her hand to her chest and appeared to wrinkle her nose. "I made her break off the engagement right away."

"*Guácala*," said Victoria with a tone of disgust. "You did the right thing, Elena."

"Of course, she did the right thing," Elena's mother said. "The milk from an Indigenous woman carries her ignorance and her fears—it passes all those horrible things to the infant. I couldn't bear to have that passed down to my own grandchildren from a father who'd been fed that kind of milk."

"Señor Knox," Victoria's father said, "it'll be a mistake and a disservice to the Mexican community if you waste your resources on such children. Those poor refugee children are incapable of learning. They were built for hard labor, and in the end, they'll serve society better if they do the work they were intended to do."

I could no longer hold in my rage.

I yanked the curtain back and stepped into the dining room.

"We're not fearful or ignorant people," I shouted.

Everyone's eyes, as big and round as dinner plates, were on me.

"We're not fearful, because thousands of people like me are fighting right now to change Mexico," I said. "We're fighting the heat, the hunger, and the pain that comes from crossing the desert to reach a better life. How can you call us fearful when our villages were burned and our fathers taken away to fight a war that lets you keep your life of luxury? How can you sit there, eat your dessert, sip your warm coffee, and call us ignorant when it's you who take opportunities away from us?"

Father Amaro stood up. "Petra, I forbid you to speak—"

"Let her speak," Mr. Knox said, standing up and raising a hand to Father Amaro.

"I'm not going to keep quiet," I said. "Not anymore. We've kept quiet for too long, and now our country is falling apart."

I looked at Victoria. Her eyes turned away from me. I wanted to reproach her for her words, but if I did, I knew I'd start crying.

Instead, I turned to Father Amaro. "You more than anyone know how terrible life is for us in Mexico. Yet you welcome these people's ideas and laugh at our struggle to survive in this new country."

Father Amaro, face red with anger, glared at me. He tightened his grip on the white napkin he held at his side. I wasn't about to let these people see me break down, so I turned and ran down the hallway feeling a fire inside me like never before.

I dashed into the kitchen, untied the strings of my apron, sat it on the table, and ran out of the church. Nothing mattered anymore. Not my life here, the church, Sister Nora's teachings, her books, my experiences—none of it mattered. I was done with everything here, with this town, and with my life in America.

I ran home in the rain as their insults continued to burn through me. Was there a curse in our mother's milk? In our blood? Was it a curse that would follow us everywhere and always make us appear as fearful people? I refused to give in to it, to accept it, but I couldn't fight it here, not in America. I didn't stand a chance here. But in Mexico, I could use the fire inside me to fight for change. I'd give my blood if necessary and show them I was not afraid.

forty-one
A MIRAGE

I arrived home, and when I opened the door, a gust of wind swirled from behind and swung it wide open. Amelia and Nina were startled. Both sat at the table, combing through a pile of uncooked beans.

"Shut that door," said Abuelita, sitting by the stove. "*Pronto!*"

I pushed the door against the strong wind.

"*Nos va dar un aire,*" said Abuelita. "If that cold air reaches us, we'll all end up sick."

After shutting the door, I walked straight to where we kept our money. I reached for the oregano plant, and my trembling hands dropped the entire plant, pot, and can into the crate below.

"Please be careful with the plants," said Abuelita.

I grabbed the small tin box from the mess and scooped up most of the scattered soil. I put the plant back together as best as I could.

"Why are you counting the money again?" asked Abuelita.

"I'm making sure you have enough," I said.

"Enough for the slate?" asked Amelia.

I glared at her without saying a word.

"*Qué te pasa*, m'ija?" Abuelita asked. "What's the matter?"

I counted the money and took some to buy a train ticket back to Mexico.

"You should have enough in this box to cover food and rent for the next four weeks."

"Petra, did Sister Nora let you go?"

Everyone stared at me with round eyes. Even Luisito had stopped nibbling on his *tamal*.

"I'm leaving," I said.

Abuelita wiped her hands across her apron. "Where to?"

My jaw felt so tight, I couldn't open my mouth to answer.

"M'ija, you're scaring me," said Abuelita. She reached for my shoulder. "What's happening?"

I took in a deep breath. "I'm going back to Mexico."

Abuelita let go of my shoulder. "No," she whispered. Her crooked fingers covered her mouth.

Amelia jumped off her chair. "Are you going back to find Papa?"

I swallowed hard. "Maybe...I don't know."

"You don't know?" Abuelita gave me a baffled look.

"I'm going back to join the rebels," I said.

Abuelita shut her eyes tight and winced. "Petra, you can't do this. You can't do this to us, to yourself."

"I've made up my mind," I said. "I came to America with dreams, and I work hard every day to make them come true, but they only move further and further away. In Mexico, if I fight with all my heart, I have a chance to make them come true."

"M'ija," said Abuelita. She clasped her hands. "Mexico's a living hell right now. Remember the violence, the terror? Don't rush into something you might—"

"It's done," I said. "I'm leaving, and I'm going to the train station right now to purchase my ticket for tomorrow."

Amelia wrapped her arms around my legs. "Don't go. You're going to be a teacher. Remember?"

I wanted to squat down and hold Amelia, but if I was going to be a tough rebel, I had to learn to shut off my emotions.

"Do you even know where to go?" said Abuelita.

"Piedras Negras," I said. "I'll start there. It's under rebel control now. Once I get there, I'll join the rebels—maybe I can even find Marietta, and as soon as I get paid, I'll start sending you money."

Abuelita tried to reach for my shoulders, but I pulled away.

"I have to get ready," I said, unwrapping Amelia's arms from my legs and pushing her away.

Amelia turned to Abuelita and clung to her instead, sobbing. My heart crumbled hearing her sobs and seeing Luisito, who looked confused. I convinced myself her suffering was necessary. It was the only way for our dreams to come true.

I walked into the next room and stood in front of the mirror.

"I have to do what's right," I whispered to myself. "And this is what's right."

I reached into my pocket, pulled out my purple scarf, and wrapped it around my neck.

"Petra," said Amelia. Her head peeked from behind the hung fabric door. I tried to soften my face for her. Amelia walked toward me, and in the dim light, I could see the fear in her face. Her small, scrunched-up shoulders reminded me of the little girl from Sister Nora's book, Cosette.

"Don't go," she said.

"Don't be so scared," I said. "I'm the one who's going. You're staying here, where it's safe. You have Nina to play with, and soon you'll start school. When it's all over, I promise I'll come back to get you all."

"Please, Petra. Please, don't go," she said. Her trembling hands tried to wipe the torrent of tears that streamed down her cheeks.

"Stop asking me to stay, Amelia." I straightened. "I don't have a choice."

"You do have a choice."

"I don't. And I don't need you to make me feel worse."

Amelia covered her face and shook as she sobbed.

"I already fulfilled Papa's promise. You're in a safe place, and now it's time I fight for my dreams."

I stopped talking. It was useless. I couldn't explain something to a little girl who'd probably become more scared and confused.

I walked around Amelia and pushed the curtain aside. Steam swirled above a pot on the stove, but Abuelita paid it no mind. She sat at the table with eyes shut as Nina stood by her and patted her gray head. Luisito, sitting on the floor and still crying, stretched his arms out to me.

Nina stared at me with sad eyes.

"I'll be back later," I said, and as I left, I tried to shut the door quickly to avoid the cool air flooding into the shack.

I trotted through puddles with knots in my stomach. I was afraid that if I kept quiet, the grasshoppers inside me would convince me to turn back and not purchase the train ticket. They'd convince me to stay.

My heart pounded harder inside my chest the closer I got to the train depot. Under the rain, the Apache statue atop the dome seemed to aim his arrow blindly into the overcast day. There was no beaming sun to guide him. I paused before stepping into the depot. There was no turning back after buying this ticket. I had no money to throw away. If I bought the ticket now, it was going to be used.

Giant, freezing drops of rain plopped on my head, pushing me to step inside.

My broken English was enough. The attendant at the window understood what I wanted and even smiled at me, but I didn't feel fulfilled nor accomplished. Not anymore. Not in this country.

My fingers wrapped around the purchased ticket, and images of the battles Marietta and Pablo had described flashed through my mind. I put a stop to the fear creeping inside me by forcing my mind to remember the names of places, of people, and of battles both had fought.

Pablo had mentioned a military group made up of nothing but women. He'd called it a regiment, and a woman general ran the whole thing. If I failed to find Marietta, I'd make my way to the women's regiment.

I walked away from the train station, ticket in hand, and looked at the city that had once given me so much hope. I walked past the infirmary. The size of the building had awed me once, but the dazzling feeling was gone. The whole city had been like a mirage in a desert, and now I was close enough to see the truth. The belief that with hard work my dreams would come true, a belief I held with all my heart, was gone.

forty-two
THE BARGAIN

I stepped onto my porch and stomped the mud off my boots. My shivering hands, deep in my pockets, touched both my baby diamond and my train ticket stamped for tomorrow morning.

I slipped inside and quickly shut the door behind me, careful to not let in much of the wind.

Abuelita rushed toward me. "She's with you, right?"

"Who?" I asked and scanned the room. Nina, sitting by Camila, had red, swollen eyes.

"It's Amelia," said Camila. Her hair was dripping. "We can't find her."

I turned to Nina. "Did you see Amelia leave?"

Nina's pouting lips quivered, and when I took a step toward her, she turned away.

"Nina," I dropped to my knees in front of her. "You're Amelia's best friend, right?"

Nina nodded, holding back tears.

"Can you tell me where she went?"

Nina shook her head.

"Look, it's raining a lot, and it's getting dark. We need to know where she—"

"Don Wong's," said Nina.

"Don Wong's? What for?" I asked.

"To get the slate."

"Did she have money?" I asked. My eyes went to the oregano plant. It looked undisturbed.

Nina shook her head. "She had her doll."

"Let's go to Don Wong's," said Camila. "Amelia's probably still there, bargaining."

"You're right," I said. "*Vamos!*"

"*Vayan con Dios*," said Abuelita and made the sign of the cross toward Camila and me.

The day had grown darker, and the rumble of the approaching storm pressed us to run faster.

Bells rang when I pushed open Don Wong's glass door.

"Amelia," I shouted.

The store was empty and dead silent. Camila and I reached the front counter.

"Don Wong," I called out to the curtain of beads that separated the store from the back living area. The curtain made soft waterfall sounds as Don Wong stepped through it.

"We're looking for Amelia. Has she been here?" I asked him.

He nodded. "One hour ago. She wanted to trade: her doll and ten cents for slate."

Don Wong's concerned eyes shifted behind him. On a shelf sat the last slate.

"I didn't accept trade, and she said she bring pecans or yellow coat, or both," said Don Wong.

"But she loved that coat," I said. "She'd never give it up."

"I say, 'No coat,'" said Don Wong, "but she say slate very important. I say ten cents, one sack of pecans, and slate is yours."

"She probably went home for pecans," said Camila.

A shiver ran through me.

"The crate," I said to Camila. "It was empty. There were no pecans in it."

"Dear God." Camila crossed herself. "You don't think she—"

Don Wong's eyes grew wider. "She step outside with gunnysack."

"Did you see which way she went?" Camila's voice trembled.

"Left," said Don Wong, pointing toward the creek.

My heart sank as a boom of thunder shook the building. The rain outside had never sounded more awful.

forty-three
THUNDER & LIGHTNING

Don Wong moved swiftly. He grabbed three looped ropes off the wall.

"She probably went to the usual patch of trees," I said.

Don Wong handed Camila and me each a lit kerosene lamp. The three of us stepped into the rain and raced toward the creek.

The storm clouds thickened and soaked up what little daylight was left. We rushed through pools of water and tall grass until lumps of mud clung to our feet and hindered our pace. Cool, wet air swirled around us, carrying a familiar stench. It was one I'd smelled before, a smell of muck, decay, and destruction.

Apart from the rumbling sky, there was a steady roar,

like the low growl of an angry animal. It grew louder the closer we got to the creek.

We reached the heart of the roar and stood on the edge of darkness. The cold rain slapped our faces. The flames in our lamps flickered in the violent wind as if trying to escape what lay ahead.

I kept my eyes locked in front of me and shouted, "I can't see any—"

A flash of lightning lit the sky, and for a moment, it was as if daylight had returned. A wave of shock hit me. The tiny creek had swollen into a monstrous river. It carried harsh noises as uprooted trees and shattered wood rushed past us.

"I walk upstream," said Don Wong. "I search patch of trees and come back." He took Camila's lamp.

My eyes adjusted to the darkness, and I tugged at Camila's arm.

"This way," I said and led Camila in the opposite direction from Don Wong, toward the patch Amelia and I frequented.

With each step, my boots sunk deeper into the mud and my heart deeper into despair.

"Amelia," Camila shouted over the roaring water.

My sense of orientation, my mind, everything was amiss. I couldn't tell where our tree patch was or where the stones Amelia used to cross the creek were.

Not far from us, a lamppost came on. Immediately, I knew where I was.

I dashed farther downstream.

"Did you see something?" said Camila.

"I'm looking for big stones, the ones Amelia hops on to get to the other side."

I lifted the oil lamp and walked to the edge of the raging waters. The rocks weren't there. They had either been swept away or were hidden under the torrent.

"Amelia!" I screamed.

Only the water's steady growl was heard. I shouted Amelia's name once more.

The wind blew again, but this time, it carried a gentle cry.

"Did you hear that?" I said to Camila. Together we ran downstream, toward the cries.

We stopped, and Camila shouted for Amelia. There was silence.

"I heard her," I said. "I swear."

"I did too," said Camila.

Lightning flashed around us. My eyes darted frantically on things flowing downstream or caught between trees.

Again, the gentle groan reached us. This time I recognized my name. My heart raced, and I narrowed my eyes to where the noise had come from.

When lightning lit the sky, a light-colored object reflected the flash. The object was wedged between the branches of a tree.

More lightning followed, and I recognized Amelia's yellow coat in a tangle of debris.

"There she is," I yelled. "Amelia!"

A bolt zigzagged above us. Its blast shook everything, even my bones. When the crashing sounds ended, Amelia's faint cries came through.

I dropped the lamp and was about to rush into the water when Camila grabbed my shoulder.

"Don't," she said. "You'll be washed away too. Stay here. I'll get Don Wong."

Camila grabbed the lamp from the ground and ran upstream, disappearing into the darkness.

I turned back to Amelia. Her cry was stronger, and she wailed my name.

"Amelia, can you hear me?" I shouted.

Her weak voice came through. "Yes."

I looked at the water. In the torrent, I could see the foam's white lining.

"I'm going to get you," I said and ran a few feet upstream.

My boots cleaved into the wet soil, causing me to trip and fall. I picked myself up. My muddy fingers fumbled to untie my bootlaces. I kicked off my boots, removed my stockings, and ran to the water.

Something hidden in the darkness stopped me from getting in. I reached out in front of me and touched a snarl of barbwire. I walked a few feet up and down. There was no way around the spiked tangle.

"Petra!" Amelia's voice shouted from the tree. "The water...it's getting higher."

I looked upstream and didn't see Don Wong or Camila's lamplights.

I turned to Amelia, sucked in my breath, and marched through the wire.

Sharp points tore into the soft flesh of my feet. I ignored the sting. The wire snagged my clothes and my skin. I yanked each limb away, ripping it free.

I dove into the water. My swimming was no match against the angry torrent. My head bobbed in the tide, and I saw Amelia's tree approaching fast. I stretched out my arms and nabbed one of its branches, just in time.

The rushing water threatened to break my grip, but slowly I managed to move along the tree. I pushed myself up and over the branch and began to crawl closer to the pile of debris, closer to Amelia.

I paused to catch my breath. "I'm almost there, Amelia."

I climbed over the pile while grasping a tree branch and reached Amelia. I threw my arms around her head and kissed it.

Amelia's arms clung to the tree, and the lower part of her legs appeared to be underwater.

"We need to move up the tree," I shouted.

"My legs," said Amelia. "They're stuck. I can't feel them."

I dug into the pile of debris around Amelia, throwing aside pieces of shattered wood, twisted metal sheets, and broken tree limbs. Bamboo sticks from crumpled birdcages stuck out of wires and branches caught around Amelia's legs. One long bamboo stick appeared to be locked in the mess. I tightened my grip around it and yanked it out.

Amelia let out a harrowing shriek.

forty-four
THE INFIRMARY

Amelia's shrill scream shook me more than the thunder blasting around us. I threw the stick down and dropped to her side.

"What's wrong?"

"My leg," Amelia cried between screams. "It burns."

The water still washed over her legs.

I grabbed her arms. "Hold my neck. I'm moving you up the tree."

Amelia howled as I lifted her and dragged her legs through the wire mesh.

I reached a higher branch and lay Amelia down on it. I tore open her coat and inspected her legs. There was a gash on one of her thighs with blood streaming out.

I pressed Amelia's thigh above the wound to slow the

bleeding. With my free hand, I grabbed the edge of my skirt to tear it. When Marietta at the rebel camp was hurt in a train accident, I'd watched a soldier bind her leg with a tourniquet, and I knew Amelia needed one. But my soaked skirt wouldn't tear, and neither would my blouse. As panic set in, I reached for my neck and felt a miracle at my fingertips.

Swiftly, I removed my scarf and secured it around Amelia's thigh.

The water rose to my legs. My body shivered, and my teeth rattled.

"Stay awake, Amelia." I said, but only moans came out of her lips.

I turned to the branches above me. We'd have to move up soon.

"Petra!" Camila shouted.

A group of about five people had gathered at the water's edge. They carried a powerful lamp and shined it into the flooded creek. Their breaths mingled with the rain.

"Here," I shouted. "Over here. I'm on the tree, with Amelia."

The light shined bright in my direction. I winced, and a hand went up to shield my eyes.

Shadows scrambled and moved swiftly. The light darted between our tree and the figure entering the water. After a moment another figure entered the water, and later a third one joined in. A rope connected them all. Soon, the first person reached us. It was Don Wong.

"Give me Amelia," he said.

I lowered Amelia to him. "She's hurt," I said. "I made a tourniquet on her leg."

Don Wong reached up for Amelia then struggled to swim to the other man. Once Amelia had reached the bank, Don Wong returned for me. As he carried me through the shallow water, I jumped from his arms and ran ashore.

"We have to get her to a doctor," I said. One man squatting by Amelia ripped a strip from his shirt.

"Yes," said Camila. "We're trying to figure out how. No one has a horse or automobile."

"Laredo Street," I said. "Someone has to be riding through there."

"In this weather?" said Camila.

"No choice," said Don Wong. "Let's go."

Don Wong, one of the men, and I ran toward the street. Camila and the other man carried Amelia.

We reached the street and within minutes saw the distant lights of an automobile. The man with us took his lamp and flashed it on and off toward the approaching beams.

The automobile drove slowly through the flooded street, and as it stopped next to us, the rain picked up. The driver was a white man who wore a police uniform and greeted us in English.

The man holding the lamp turned to Don Wong. "*Hablas ingles?* Do you speak English?"

Don Wong shook his head.

"*Yo hablo ingles,*" I shouted and wedged myself between Don Wong and the other man. "I speak English."

The policeman stared with round eyes.

"My sister," I said in English. "She has cut. Much blood comes out. We need doctor."

"Where's your sister?" The policeman asked.

I pointed behind me. By this time the man carrying Amelia was approaching. The policeman jumped out of his automobile and rushed to open the back door. He patted the back seat, and the man laid Amelia on it. The policeman motioned for me to sit next to her before shutting the door.

"Be safe, Petra," called Camila.

The policeman began to drive, and I looked over at Amelia. A sturdy fabric had replaced my purple scarf around her leg, and her eyes were still shut. I pushed Amelia's wet hair away from her face.

The policeman said something, but he spoke so fast, I couldn't understand. His hand reached back. It held a small blanket.

I wrapped Amelia. "We're going to a doctor, *chiquita*. They'll make you feel better."

The automobile jerked to a stop at the Santa Rosa infirmary's entrance. The policeman rushed inside, and within seconds three men dressed in white came out and placed Amelia on a stretcher. I ran behind them into the building, wincing at the bright lights.

When my eyes adjusted, horror flashed through me as I saw Amelia. Her skin was as white as the men's uniforms, and her cracked lips were tinted blue. Her yellow coat was covered in mud and blood.

An old, bearded man in spectacles wearing a white uniform put his hand on her neck. His eyes widened. He shouted words in English to the men, too fast for me to grasp. The old man pushed a door open, and the men carrying Amelia rushed through it.

I feared the worst and screamed. "Amelia!"

At the door a hand grabbed my shoulder and pulled me back. Amelia's limp arm dangled from the stretcher, and the men raced down the hallway and turned a corner.

I jerked myself free and took another step. "Amelia!"

More hands grabbed at my shoulders and my arms.

"*Suéltenme!* Let me go!" I snapped at the people dragging me back. I reached for the doorjambs and clung to them. My knuckles turned white.

"It's not supposed to be this way," I shouted in Spanish, not caring if people understood or not. "It's supposed to be me! Not you, Amelia!"

Two men attempted to pry my fingers off the doorjambs. I kicked at them and elbowed the people behind me.

A firm voice shouted over the ruckus.

"Petra!"

I loosened my grip and turned to the familiar voice.

A group of nuns dressed in white robes and white habits had gathered near me. Behind them was one with sapphire eyes—Sister Nora.

I let go of the door and ran to her.

Sister Nora wrapped her arms around me.

"What...what are you doing here?" I asked. My hands clutched her wet coat, not wanting to let go.

"The entire train system shut down because of the rain. I couldn't make it to Leon Springs," Sister Nora said. "When I got back to the church, Father Amaro complained about you, and I worried. I was about to look for you at your home when the infirmary called for me, needing my help."

Sister Nora wiped the water off her face that dripped from her soaked hair. "What happened?"

I buried my head on her shoulder and let myself break down. I could barely speak through sobs.

"I'm a failure," I said. Every tear burned no matter how hard I pressed myself against Sister Nora. "I failed to find Papa, failed to take care of my sister, and now she's dying because of me."

I pulled back and looked into her tender eyes. "Amelia wanted me to stay but I refused. I didn't stay with her like Róisín would have stayed with you."

"Petra." Sister Nora's voice was firm but loving. She cupped my face with her hands. "Amelia's in good hands. And you're a wonderful sister."

I wanted to believe Sister Nora, but every time I shut my eyes, I saw Amelia's pale skin and darkened lips. I had failed Papa. I had failed my promise. And I had failed the people I loved the most. The weight of shame and guilt brought me to my knees, and Sister Nora knelt beside me. She embraced me and rocked along with my pain.

forty-five

A DREAM STATE

I awoke to the gentle sound of a flutter. I lay on my side, curled up. Across from me, a lamp's short flame burned steady, though its faint light was not enough to ebb the darkness around me. I shut my eyes, and again, the whisper of tiny wings came to me.

It was a moth, and it chased the small flame erratically. It whirled and zigzagged around the lamp's glow only to crash hard against its glass. It did this over and over as if its life depended on reaching the light. The staunch little thing continued to fly until it found the gap at the top of the glass. Hungry for the light, the moth plunged down, straight to its demise.

I closed my eyes, and in my head, I still heard the fluttering.

Other senses awakened. The taste of lemon lingered in my mouth, and when I reached to rub my nose, my hand smelled of mud and blood. Amelia's name fired through my head. My heart pounded, and I sat up.

"Amelia!" I shouted into the darkness. Only the sounds of my shallow breaths echoed in the small room.

I jumped to my feet and saw the bright light that seeped through the bottom of a door. I rushed to it and pushed it open.

I winced at the glare but still caught sight of the long, empty hallway. Its stark white walls matched the bandages on my arms, hands, and feet. My clothes, covered in grime, were tattered and bloodstained.

"Amelia!" My voice echoed in the cold hallway.

I limped down the corridor toward the brighter end. My body shivered, and my knees wobbled. The bottoms of my feet stung with every step.

"Amelia!" I shouted again.

A nun peeked her head out near the end of the hallway and hushed me.

"Sister Nora?" I asked.

The nun shook her head and motioned for me to wait before disappearing.

Within moments Sister Nora's voice flowed down the hallway. "Petra." She rushed toward me. "How are you?"

"Where's Amelia?" I asked. "I need to see her. Please."

Sister Nora reached for my shoulder. "Amelia's sleeping now, but I'll take you to her."

Sister Nora led me through a maze of corridors. Some were bright, others were dim, and most had a stench that turned my stomach.

We reached a wide door, and Sister Nora whispered into my ear, "She's in here."

I entered a long, somber room and walked down the middle between two rows of beds.

Whispers, coughs, and moans resonated through the room. Amelia's bed was at the very end, near a row of windows that let the predawn light come through. A tingling sensation swept over me when I saw her. She slept without a sound.

My eyes welled up. "Her color is back," I said.

Amelia's head was bandaged. Her face, legs, and arms were cut and bruised. I reached for her hand and noticed torn fingernails. Some had been completely ripped away. She had fought hard to save herself. She was a fierce little girl with a big noble heart, and I had let her down.

I knelt beside her bed, and still holding her hand, I broke down.

Sister Nora patted my shoulder. "What's the matter?"

My chest tightened with guilt. "She almost died because of my selfishness."

"Child, you saved her life." Sister Nora knelt next to me. "Look at me."

I turned to her.

"The tourniquet you made, it worked."

My eyes fell back on Amelia. She slept in a peaceful silence. Her serene expression was like Mama's during her wake.

"What if she never wakes up?" I asked.

"Amelia's sedated. She'll wake up later today."

"I said awful things to her when all she wanted to do was protect me."

I turned to Sister Nora. "The only reason I wanted to go back to Mexico was because during yesterday's dinner..." A lump that had formed in my throat wouldn't let words come out. "Everyone was trying to convince Mr. Knox to open the school elsewhere. They want the school to be for girls like Victoria and Elena, not for children like Amelia and me."

"Petra, I know Mr. Knox. As a matter of fact, I saw him before coming here. He told me everything. He also shared how impressed he was with your courage to speak up."

"He told you that?" I wiped away tears.

"He did. And he's excited to interview you for the teaching position."

"I can't do that interview," I said. "I can't teach what I don't know."

"What are you talking about, child?"

"After you left, I thought I'd found Papa's name in the paper. It turns out I hadn't read it right. I read *Alonso* instead of *Alfonso*."

"M'ija, that was just a small oversight. I've done that plenty of times. But it's you who needs to believe this. It's you who needs to believe that you're strong and courageous. It's you who needs to trust how capable you are."

I turned to Amelia and cupped her hand between mine. "I thought I'd have a better chance fighting for my dreams in Mexico than here."

"You've already won half the battle. You're here, in America."

Sister Nora stood, grabbed a chair, and brought it close to me. She sat and leaned into me.

"Nothing in life comes easy or is perfect," said Sister Nora. "The sooner you learn this, the easier it'll be to move beyond setbacks without making rash decisions."

"I lied too," I said, lowering my gaze. "I lied to you, to my family, and I feel terrible."

"What did you lie about?"

"I always said I wanted to go back and find Papa, but in reality, I'm scared. I don't know how or where to look for him. I save the money because I'm scared of losing my job. I'm scared of not making it in this country. I'm afraid of everything, and when I wanted to put an end to my fears, the worst happened. The sign on the bridge had it right, I am a person of fear."

"That sign is as outdated as the beliefs of Father Amaro's guests. People like them cling to their old views like a cactus hangs on to a raindrop."

Between tears, I chuckled at Sister Nora's comparison. "How do you know?"

"Because I cook dinners for them and have to listen to their shenanigans as I serve them."

"I meant about the cacti."

"Oh." Sister Nora slapped her leg. "I spent time in the Mexican desert and saw how precious droplets are to those plants, especially when the powerful sun comes out. The cacti get desperate and grow thorns to capture every drop before it evaporates forever."

I could see how these rich people had grown thorns, because when I'd gotten close to Victoria, her thorns had pricked me.

"Don't fall for the belief that you're a child of fear, otherwise you'll be like them," Sister Nora said. "Let go of the past because it owes you nothing, and embrace the good things in front of you before they vanish."

I turned to Amelia and gently caressed her face. Her lips twitched.

"Is she in pain?" I asked.

"No, she's resting."

A nun approached us. "Sister Nora, you're needed downstairs."

"I'll be there in a minute," Sister Nora said.

The nun gave me a smile and turned away.

"Do you remember the books in my trunk? Remember Galileo, Copernicus, and Darwin?"

I nodded.

"These men, in their hearts, knew what they wanted and stuck with it. When the world wouldn't accept their beliefs, they never budged."

"Just like Marietta," I said, "the woman soldier I met in Mexico."

"Yes. People like her put a higher value on their beliefs and on the life of others than their own lives, and they'll fight to their death to make the world a better place."

Sister Nora used her fingers to comb my hair back then lifted my chin. "You escaped the revolution, Petra, but life will always have its battles, no matter who you are or where you go."

Sister Nora kissed my head before walking away.

I squeezed Amelia's hand. She was a little warrior who had fought by my side all along.

"I love you, Amelia," I said. "You're the best sister."

When I pecked her cheek, her lips released a small sigh.

"I'm not going anywhere," I said. "My fight is here with you and Luisito. You've been the brave soldier, watching out for me. Now, I need you to fight and get better."

A gust of wind pushed against the windows, rattling them. Amelia's eyes fluttered open and drifted to them.

"Papa?" she said in a faint voice.

"Amelia," I said, overjoyed to hear her delicate voice.

She lifted her head. "It's Papa."

"No. Papa's not here."

The wind gushed again, and this time, it swung the windowpane near us wide open. Every curtain flew up.

"Ehecatl," Amelia cried out toward the wind. Her eyes winced.

A nun rushed to shut the window.

"It's Ehecatl," Amelia whispered. "He's bringing Papa." She lay her head back down and closed her eyes.

My heart thumped in my ears.

"Amelia." I shook her gently. Had she seen Papa's spirit? Was he dead? Had he come to take Amelia away?

I raised my voice. "Amelia!" I grabbed her shoulders and shook her. "Stay with us. Don't go."

A nun came to me. "She's sedated. Let her rest."

I nodded nervously. "Here," I whispered to Amelia. "I'll put my black rock in your hand so you can feel closer to Papa."

I reached into my pocket but didn't feel it. Instead, I pulled out shreds of wet grass and mud. I reached deep into the other pocket. My baby diamond was gone.

Kneeling, I lowered my head over Amelia's hand and sobbed. It was the last thing I had of Papa, and now it was gone. All I was left with were memories of him.

I whispered to Amelia, "Remember when Papa used to come home from work? Remember how we used to race to meet him? Sometimes I'd beat you, and sometimes I pretended to step on a sharp rock to let you win. And no matter how much black dust was on his face or on his clothes, we'd always cling to him."

The furrow in Amelia's brow faded.

"And that song he'd always whistle—'*Adiós Mamá Carlota*'—remember how we'd beg him to sing it before bedtime? He said the song made him feel strong."

I hummed the song to Amelia and caressed her hair. The song flowed through me. Papa had been right. The song was powerful. It made me see a bright future full of hope.

Behind me, a low hushing sound mimicked my singing. I smiled, not surprised Sister Nora knew the song.

I turned to see behind me, but it wasn't Sister Nora. I stood slowly, certain I was dreaming.

"M'ija," said the raspy voice.

It was Papa.

forty-six

TAKING AIM

I threw myself into Papa's arms. His clothes were wet but smelled like spring showers. Papa had never felt bigger or stronger under my arms.

I pulled back. "How..." I couldn't catch my breath fast enough to finish the question.

One of my hands cradled his face and the other caressed it, making sure he was real. The small scar on his chin was still there, but new, bigger scars marked his face.

"How did you..." I stopped myself. It didn't matter how he'd gotten here—if he'd read the paper or if someone told him about my announcement. He was here with me now. "What happened to you?"

"I fought," Papa said, "I fought to get back to you. I was in Ojinaga, and the rebels were surrounding us.

I didn't want to fight them and decided to cross the river and hundreds of miles through the desert for the opportunity to find you. Lucky for me, Pablo found me at a refugee camp out west."

Pablo stood a few feet behind Papa with his arm around Abuelita, who sobbed into her shawl. Despite her eyes being full of tears, they beamed with love, joy, and relief all braided into one.

"It's a long story," Papa said, "but I'll tell it to you in due time."

Papa's eyes beamed as he ran his hand over my face. "You've grown so much. You have your mother's eyes, you know?"

I blushed, grabbing his hand and resting it on my face to feel his rough palms.

"I'm sorry, m'ija." A tear escaped Papa's eye. "Your abuela told me all you went through, and I'm so sorry you had to go through all this without me."

"Don't, Papa." I leaned toward him and embraced him. "Don't be sorry. I made a promise to you. You kept yours and I—"

My throat knotted up again. I turned to Amelia then back to Papa.

"I'm the one who should be sorry," I said. "I didn't keep my promise."

Papa looked up. "What do you mean?"

"Look at her, Papa." My voice broke. "Amelia's here because of me."

Papa shook his head, "She's here in America and in this hospital because you've saved her life. You kept your promise." Papa raised my chin. "I can't think of a braver person, Petra, and I couldn't be prouder of you."

Papa embraced me once more. "Thank you for keeping your promise."

I squeezed Papa back and saw that Abuelita had broken away from Pablo. She waddled quickly toward Papa and stretched her arms to embrace us both. "I can't stop hugging you, m'ijo," she said to Papa under her breath. "I can't stop."

Papa, Abuelita, and I gripped at each other, almost afraid to let go. It'd been a long time since I'd felt this much comfort, this much affection and hope for the future, and as we stood together, my eyes glanced outside. The sunlight had broken through the heavy clouds, and once again, the Apache atop the dome had a steady aim at the rising light. And so did I.

SPRING 1914

THREE MONTHS LATER

forty-seven
THE THRESHOLD

I took a seat in a wooden chair and smoothed out the skirt of my sailor suit. I straightened the bow on my hair and took a deep breath. My sweaty palms held Sister Nora's character letter and a small red book she'd given me for my thirteenth birthday. It was a good luck gift, she claimed, but for me it was proof that my bare-foot dreams had started to come true. The book had become a part of me like my black rock and my purple scarf.

Nervous but unafraid, I raised my eyes to the clock on the wall.

"You're early," said a lady in English. She sat behind a desk. "He'll be with you shortly."

I acknowledged her with a smile and read the sign

nailed to the shut door across from me: MR. W. J. KNOX, SCHOOL DIRECTOR.

I turned to the window behind me. Outside, sunlight poured over a park. I squinted my eyes, and on a nearby bench sat Sister Nora. She had promised me a nice meal at the café to celebrate my meeting with Mr. Knox.

A week from now, Amelia and Luisito would start going to the new school and Papa would start a new job that allowed him to spend weekends with us. Now that my siblings would be gone most of the day, Abuelita would have more time to rest and cook Pablo's favorite meals every time he visited.

At the church, everything was quiet with Father Amaro gone. He'd been sent back to Mexico. The street by the church had been widened, and a modern concrete bridge had replaced the old iron one. Gone too was the outdated sign that had caused me much turmoil.

"Ms. Petra Luna," said the young lady. She held the door open and motioned me to go in.

"Thank you," I said.

For a moment, I stood on the threshold and gazed at the man sitting behind the desk. I didn't bother to reach into my pocket or for my neck. I no longer needed my baby diamond nor my scarf for strength. I felt complete, as if all the light in the universe beamed through me.

In one breath, I absorbed the light around me and stepped in.

Note from the Author

Writing historical fiction has many rewards, and one of them is getting to know the era, the people, and the culture being studied. But when the research validates a family story, the rewards are even more profound.

The character of Petra Luna was inspired by the experiences my great-grandmother, Güelita Juanita, endured as a child during the Mexican Revolution. In my research for this book, I was awestruck to find out how close my great-grandmother's stories were to the newspaper articles I read from 1913. Her detailed descriptions of crossing into the United States and her stay at the refugee camp were confirmed with every word I read. She was tremendously thankful to the United States for opening its gates on the bridge over the Rio Grande River and for providing safety to her and her family after having escaped the Federales. She was filled with gratitude when she spoke about her time in the refugee camp and claimed that she'd never eaten so well in her entire life, up to that point.

Like Petra Luna and her family, my great-grandmother's family was given the option to return to Mexico or stay in America, where she and her father would be guaranteed work. Juanita, being the oldest sibling, talked it over with her father and after much consideration, they decided to return to their home country. "Mexico was our homeland," she would say. "It was our job to nurture her back to health." Upon their return to Mexico, Güelita Juanita and her family discovered that everything had been burned to the ground—homes, farmlands, entire villages—and found themselves starting over again from the bottom with nothing but the clothes on their backs. This is where Petra's story diverges from my family history. While the story of my family's return to Mexico was interesting, I was intrigued by the lives of the immigrants who decided to make a new life in America and decided this would be Petra's story.

Mexico was my birthplace and at a very young age, my mother and I moved to San Antonio, Texas. I have since called the Alamo City my home. In my research, I was fascinated to learn that 30,000 refugees had immigrated to San Antonio during the Mexican Revolution. I read about the many struggles these refugees endured, from housing shortages to the lack of work opportunities, all while experiencing the shock of a new culture and language. It didn't take me long to realize that these were challenges Petra Luna would have to overcome if it meant keeping her promise.

My research of old San Antonio gave me a new and refreshing perspective on the city I love so much. I found out about the origins of "Little Mexico," the glamour of the chili queens, and the floods that ravaged San Antonio in 1913. I gained a deeper understanding of things I had always felt close to but knew very little about, like my childhood corner store at S. Flores and Cevallos in San Antonio. The store, closed now for many years, still displays the name "Wong Store." When I was a child, Don Wong, the owner, was a Chinese immigrant who spoke Spanish and always made sure I received my pilón, just like Amelia. In my research, I learned of the many Chinese who'd been living in Mexico and had escaped the wrath of the revolution to settle in San Antonio.

As a child, I attended W.J. Knox Elementary School and at the time, no one there knew the story behind the man my school had been named for and whose vintage picture hung in the main hallway. His friendly eyes seemed to tell me I could achieve anything I set my mind to, and in return, I'd whisper to him that I wanted to make him proud one day. In my research, I learned about a teacher who wanted to make a difference in the lives of Mexican immigrant children, like Petra and Amelia. His vision was to provide English classes, early education, recreational sports, and create opportunities for poor children to attend school. He established the Navarro School in the heart of San Antonio's Mexican neighborhood and went as far as to use his own money to purchase books and supplies for children who couldn't afford it. I was amazed when I made the connection between this teacher, Wilbur John Knox and W. J. Knox, whose picture had encouraged me so much as a child. It's a testament to Mr. Knox's vision that I, who benefited so much from his efforts, grew up to write a book that would touch upon his vision. I recognize his powerful impact on me and my community, and I'm honored to acknowledge him, his compassionate spirt, and his friendly eyes.

I attended J.C. Harris Middle School (named after a writer!) and graduated from G.W. Brackenridge High School in San Antonio. In my research, I discovered that Mr. Knox indeed struggled to find funding for his innovative school, and it was Mr. Brackenridge, a local banker and philanthropist, who believed in Mr. Knox's vision and gave him the funds needed to carry out his plan for the new school.

In the story, Petra mentions a store named C.C. Butt Grocery, which during that time really existed in a town not far from San Antonio. This family-owned grocery store has since grown and is now known to Texans as HEB. To me, and to many other people, HEB is family. For my first year of college, the only scholarship I received was from HEB and many of my life lessons as a kid were learned inside an HEB. Like Mr. Knox who dedicated his life to serving the community, HEB has also had an incredible impact on communities throughout Texas since its founding by Mrs. Florence Butt in the early 1900's.

I've witnessed many successes attributed to individual hard work but many of these triumphs were made possible by a community who supported and believed in the individual. My community played a vital role in helping me accomplish my dreams, and for that I am forever grateful. One of my passions is meeting people, getting to know them, and discovering what makes us alike. I truly believe we're more similar than we think and when we focus on these similarities, our community thrives. While we should celebrate our uniqueness, we must also unite to celebrate our commonalities. When we do this, we foster a power that drives us to accomplish the impossible.

Acknowledgments

Historical fiction writers build worlds using bricks of historical facts. The mortar, the substance that fills the gaps and holds the bricks together, comes from our hearts and imagination. I am eternally grateful to my mother, Lorena Chapa, for the many family stories she shared. Her stories delivered the fear and despair and the joys and triumphs of my people not found in history books or archived newspapers. With every story she shared, she supplied many of the raw materials I've used for this book.

I'd like to thank Joan Ammi Paquette with Erin Murphy Literary Agency for helping me put Petra Luna out in the world. A big thank-you to my wonderful editor, Wendy McClure. Your friendship, guidance, and amazing insight allows me to tackle and overcome the "sophomore book" jitters. I'm also very grateful for the dedicated Sourcebooks team members, including BrocheAroe Fabian, Heather Moore, Ashlyn Keil, Margaret Coffee, Caitlin Lawler, Emily Luedloff, Valerie Pierce, Tiffany Shultz, Maryn Arreguín, and to include the many, many talented people who worked behind the scenes to bring this book to life. You are all amazing professionals. Many thanks to the brilliant illustrator John Jay Cabuay.

A writer's world, though lonely at times, is full of many friends who from a distance encourage you and support you. I want to thank my friends (and very talented writers) Holly Schindler, Laura Resau, Daniel Aleman, Payal Doshi, Margie Longoria, Maria E. Andreu, Francisco X. Stork, and Natalie Aguirre. I also want to thank the incredible librarians Rae Longest in Alvin, TX, Mary R. Lanni in Colorado, Therese Gordon at Oakdale Elementary (Toledo, OH), Douglas Keel at Marrs Magnet Center (Omaha, NE), and Norma Montalvo at San Antonio Independent School District for believing in Petra Luna from the start.

I'm enormously indebted to the many wonderful

booksellers who have contributed to the growth of my career from the start. These include Brien López (Children's Book World), Anastasia McKenna, Kell Austin, and Claudia Maceo (The Twig), Hannah Amrollahi (The Bookworm), Denise Phillips (Gathering Volumes), John and Michelle Cavalier (Cavalier Books), Lauren Silva (Second Star to the Right), and Lady Smith (Snail on the Wall). Thank you for your encouragement and advice and for connecting me to many wonderful readers.

I'd like to thank friends and family who provided much warmth and encouragement during my busy and chaotic days: Angelina Garza, Bill Dobbs, Natasha Orlando, Arianné Villanueva, and Laura Chapa. And to Tom and Pat Dobbs for their continued support.

Finally, to Annabella and Nate. Thank you for filling my life with joy and meaning. I love you.

And really finally, to my husband Mike. Thank you for always being there.

About the Author

Photo © Katherine O. Ryan

Alda P. Dobbs received a Pura Belpré Honor and a nomination for the Texas Bluebonnet Award for her debut novel *Barefoot Dreams of Petra Luna.* Both that book and *The Other Side of the River* are drawn from experiences Alda's great-grandmother endured during the Mexican Revolution in 1913. Alda was born in a small town in northern Mexico and moved to San Antonio, Texas as a child. She studied physics and worked as an engineer before pursuing her love of storytelling. She is as passionate about connecting children to their past, their communities, different cultures, and nature as she is about writing.

Alda lives with her husband and two children outside Houston, Texas. To learn more about her, visit aldapdobbs.com.